*The
Right
Thing
to Do*

The Right Thing to Do

Josephine

Gattuso

Hendin

David R. Godine
Publisher
Boston

First published in 1988 by
DAVID R. GODINE, PUBLISHER, INC.
Horticultural Hall
300 Massachusetts Avenue
Boston, Massachusetts 02115

Library of Congress Cataloging-in-Publication Data
Hendin, Josephine.
The right thing to do.
I. Title
PS3558.E49513R54   1988   813'.54   86-45529
ISBN 0-87923-639-6

FIRST EDITION
Printed in the United States of America

It is possession of the good that causes delight
whether we are conscious of possessing it actually,
or call to mind our previous possession,
or hope to possess it in the future.

Thomas Aquinas

*The
Right
Thing
to Do*

One

"Drink your ginger ale, Nino, it's getting warm," Laura said, grumpily turning to shake her finger at Maria's body. "Even dead," she accused, "you're giving us trouble."

"Can't you speak to her with some respect, now that she's gone?" Nino asked.

"Respect? You could always count on your sister to say the wrong thing. Marrying that bum who left her every time she got pregnant. Six kids, six times she takes him back. A Sicilian woman should have known better. When you try to reason with her, what does she say? What did you say, Maria?" she demanded. "Did you say, 'Maybe you've got a point,' or 'I've learned my lesson'? No! you said, 'He really can play the mandolin!'"

"Will you stop talking to her that way?" Nino pleaded, settling his foot on the worn green hassock in front of him. Since the priest had walked out on them, even the furniture seemed shamed.

Laura continued. "She had no business telling that Irish

priest who came to give the last rites that all religions were the same. Why couldn't she keep her mouth shut and let him give her the rites? She knows these young priests have no heart. They don't give a damn about anything but the book."

"She only said that because Elena was in the room. You know she's a Protestant," Nino answered weakly. What else could he say? It was bad enough to be dead without having to be an embarrassment on top of it. It wasn't clear whether Maria would be ashamed or not—that was the trouble. I'm the one who feels it, Nino thought bitterly. It was he who had gotten up in the middle of the night, he who faced the Queens BMT with no coffee and climbed the stairs of the El at Grand Avenue, stairs that stretched above him like Everest: no place for a man with a bad leg. And all for the measly two-stop trip to the end of the line at Ditmars Boulevard, where the night wind was chilly from the river and the stairway down was so shrouded in shadows and so pitted with rusty craters that it gaped like an invitation to fall all the way to another country.

It *was* another country, he had realized. The shops on Ditmars, heavily gated and sealed against the night, showed that. What had happened to the neighborhood? The old bakery with good bread and the pastry shop with its dripping rumcake were gone. Now electronics stores with ridiculous names barricaded themselves behind solid metal walls as though they expected to be attacked by foreign troops. Nino had limped, heartbroken over Maria, past the once-neat attached houses. White paint-peels curled into the wind from some; others were eerily stained with mud and graffiti; some houses had aluminum siding that revealed ball-shaped dents under the harsh street lights. The rose arbors that had graced house after house seemed overgrown with climbing vines and weeds. Where the Ristorante Venezia had been, there was a gaudy fast-food place featuring hamburgers with nauseatingly cute names. What could that food taste like, he wondered, trying to blot out his memories of feastlike lunches at the Venezia. He and Maria would talk about the old country while the kids, growing bored, ate and went outside to play catch. They were hard to bear, the thoughts of her: the walks he took with her and the kids along Shore Boulevard, the hours they spent watching the river lap against the gray-brown beach, the pebbles washing back and forth in the current while the kids held throwing contests.

True, there had been dead fish washed up now and then. But not the way it was after the Con Ed and municipal sewage plants had been built. They had crushed Steinway Creek between them. They're as bad for the nose as the eyes, Maria had said. But still, the air had been sweet from the grass of Astoria Park; the view of Riker's Island against the graceful curves of the Hell Gate Bridge was lovely; the concrete mass of Manhattan loomed, huge and miraculous, across the water. And all around you there were the well-kept row houses of people you could understand without even knowing their names. Who could have had better sights, better days? Laura always blamed him for going to Maria every time he took out Gina. You can't cope with your daughter alone, she used to say, but so what? Gina had her cousins to play with, and Maria was good to talk to. There was a woman who appreciated him, who could really listen. Laura had always resented her. What was he supposed to do, give up his sister?

"Who ever heard of such a thing?" Laura persisted. "Six children, five Catholics and one Protestant," she concluded, shaking her head in disgust.

"Mama was a Protestant," Nino came back.

"She doesn't count. Spitting at the Bishop of Palermo instead of kissing his ring doesn't make you a Protestant."

"She did it because the Church never did anything to help . . . ," Nino said, his voice trailing into hopelessness.

"Did it help the poor that she spit? Did it make the Church any different? No Neapolitan would have spit, let me tell you. She had to leave town because no one would marry her after that. Now no one will bury her daughter," she concluded triumphantly. " 'Well,' " she went on, mimicking the Irish priest, " 'since you believe *that*, you're not in need of the rites of the Holy Roman Church,' and he snaps his book shut. Damn him to hell." She could still hear her grandmother, almost patient in her bitterness, tell of the Irish priests who made the Italians say Mass in the basement while they kept the chapel to themselves. Here in Astoria at the end of the BMT it should have been different. But she could imagine the nuns, heavy in layers of swirling habits, standing like black bats at the door of the graceful gray church, their rosaries and crucifixes wound about them like garrison belts.

Everywhere they had gone, the priest's words seemed to follow them. They had walked Astoria, all morning, all afternoon, hobbling past the three-story brick buildings on Grand Avenue, where neatly kept stores displayed engagement rings and watches like holy relics and fruit stands with sawdust floors spilled baskets of peaches and tomatoes onto the sidewalk. The air was laced with rich smells, the odor of provolone cheese in summer, of hot bread, of sweet basil softening the exhaust fumes. But the priest's words seemed to cut, to flatten out every bit of life. At every church they came to, everyone asked the same question: Why didn't the priest from her parish give her the rites? No matter what they answered, they kept getting sent back to the Irishman. They all stuck together, these priests, like doctors in a malpractice suit.

Nino tapped his cane against the floor. "I should go out to try some more churches," he said.

"There aren't any more around here," Laura pointed out, her hand waving over all of the Ditmars Fountains development houses, where Maria had rented a small apartment. The buildings did seem to huddle together, dark, wine-colored brick walk-ups five stories high, fringed with tattered bushes. Here and there the meager lawns were graced by grape arbors, fig trees, tiny vegetable gardens planted by tenants who could never see the point of grass, of growing what couldn't be eaten.

"It's not so easy to make it up and down five flights of stairs," Nino said. "We'll wait until the others get here. Anyway," his voice softened, "she shouldn't be left alone now." He sat back in his chair, fingering his glass of ginger ale. "She was so good," he said, mostly to himself. "So gentle."

"Who?" Laura asked.

"My sister. Maria. Who else?" Nino answered. "She loved music. She knew it was near the end, but she wanted to go out listening to Puccini."

"That's all she ever did, even before she was ready to leave," Laura persisted. "She listened to *Madame Butterfly* and got pregnant." Her anger was gone, but still she continued. "She didn't even have the ambition to think of dying like an American, in a hospital."

Nino limped over to Maria's record table and began thumbing through her worn albums. The maple console that housed the phonograph had three legs and a prop made of three Queens Yellow Pages. Nino lingered over *Madame Butterfly* and *Turandot*. He flipped past *La Bohème*, muttering. "One melody doesn't make an opera. I never agreed with you about Puccini," he said to Maria. He frowned at how new the cover of *Nabucco* looked. He had bought it for her years ago.

"She wouldn't like that," Laura said. "Why don't you play something she likes?"

"The more you hear, the more you appreciate the better things," Nino said patiently, putting the record on. He limped to the scarred wooden rocker with flowers painted on it, their stems intertwined, and sat down heavily. It was a sunny room, bright in the late afternoon sun. On the windowsill was a flowerpot stained with a crusted white powder that seemed to have worked its way through the pot wall from the plant itself. The plant boasted two shriveled buds; its leaves had turned silvery gray from dehydration. How long had Maria been too far gone to water it?

Nino rocked to the music. Maria's crochet work was everywhere in the room; the rose pattern she had liked had been worked into doilies that covered all the surfaces. The table next to him had one covering its scratched glass top. The scratches almost blended into the lacework. Had she thought of that? One of the legs had been fixed with wood putty, but never stained. Half-finished, Nino sighed, struggling to hear the music over the sound of the El. He strained to make out the details of an oil painting done by Angelo, Maria's youngest son. It was filled with greens and blues, but it wasn't clear whether it was a field or the ocean. No waves, Nino concluded; it must be the country.

The table next to the chair was cluttered with pictures. There was Freddie in a Marine uniform, a powerful, good-looking boy. Next to him was a plasticized letter, describing his heroism before he was killed in action in Vietnam. Nino sighed. He had died like a man, Freddie. Maria had been through a lot; he trembled, remembering that Freddie was only nineteen when he died. There were pictures of almost everyone: Laura and he stood, serious, unsmiling, on their wedding day. What a figure she had in those days! There was one of him with his brother Aldo's son, Vinnie. He looked at the picture closely. Vinnie was about fifteen; his boyish face grinned from under the beak of a New York Yankees baseball cap. I gave him that cap, Nino remembered.

It was after Aldo died and Vinnie adopted me as a father.
That must be thirty years ago.

It seemed as though his life was there, in these framed
pictures, placed at random without meaning or order unless
his memory could provide it. There was a photo of Maria at
sixteen, her beautiful face looking directly into the camera.
There he was with his daughter, Gina. She was about four
years old, wearing a bonnet and holding a catcher's mitt he
had given her. What a lousy catcher she was! The ball was
always hitting her in the face—she had no idea of distances.
She wasn't a quitter, though. She would keep trying. Then
there was one of her at the Astoria pool with Angelo. She
was holding a medal she had won in a city swimming contest.
That was the year she stopped eating. The more spaghetti
he ate, he thought sourly, the more she took up swimming
and starving. He had to admit she could swim, but what did
it take to swim?

Then he saw Gina had given Maria her yearbook picture.
"To Aunt Maria with all my love," she had written in the
corner. His copy had said, "To Dad with all my love." He
frowned. They couldn't both be true! She had really liked
Maria. What a combination—his happy-go-lucky sister and
his calculating daughter. She had liked Maria for the wrong
reasons. She thought Maria didn't care about things that were
important to him. It made him more determined to bury
Maria correctly. He looked at Gina's portrait. She was looking
directly into the camera, lips without a smile, as though she
alone had a sense of the seriousness of life. Her hair was
brushed back from her face and fell in loose waves to her
shoulders. She wore a simple dark blouse with a wide V neck
that exposed her shoulders. It was striking, austere. The
features were delicate, shapely, but what drew him was her
eyes and the clear expression in them. She was out to take

everything on, that's what those eyes said, Nino thought.
Large, dark, almond-shaped, intense, full of will. That was
the worst—the confidence, the determination. It was no way
for a young girl to look.

Next to the table there was a straw basket, woven in the
shape of a duck, painted green with an orange beak. The
tag, MADE IN CHINA, was still attached. The duck was filled
with cards. He opened one, idly trying to get his mind off
Gina. "In Loving Memory," it said in fancy red writing. "Our
Lady of Blessed Peace Church certifies that Giovanni Cabo-
tini" —a blank space had been filled in with the name of
Maria's husband, in neat blue ink— "has been enrolled as a
Member in the Purgatorial Society of Our Lady of Blessed
Peace for one year and as such will share in the masses
celebrated on behalf of its members at Our Lady of Blessed
Peace Church." Mass cards, he saw, thumbing through them,
in all sizes, from different churches. The church charged ten
dollars for tiny ones, but better ones that were certified and
bound in dark blue or green plastic, with gold-tooled designs,
could be bought for five dollars from the lady who ran the
local liquor store. Who better to understand the need to
organize for repentant sinners! He saw that Maria had bought
a card from her. He read through all of them. Giovanni had
been a member of fourteen purgatorial societies. He had
needed a lot of prayer; he had gotten it. Now his year was
long since up. Where was he now?

Funny that Maria had saved all the cards from his funeral.
But, after all, that only proved his point: she cared about
things like that. Her kind of faith was hard to keep up. It
had taken a lot of blows: the time when her daughter-in-law
who taught in a Catholic school was fired when she asked for
maternity leave. Maria had screamed, "No birth control, no
abortion, and no time off for your babies when you have
them! Where is their decency?" Yet it had come to nothing,

like his attempts to get her buried. You harden yourself to the Church's hypocrisy, inhumanity, Nino thought, rocking with the mournful music, and then all of a sudden it hits. Gina would get the wrong idea from it. He had to bury Maria the right way.

There it was, he thought, losing himself in the music, his favorite part. There was nothing like this. Verdi knew what he was doing. There were the Jews, helpless, captives of King Nebuchadnezzar. No luck, those people. No better than slaves. Still, Nino thought, they were not really enslaved because they never considered where they were their real place. It was just the location of a temporary ordeal, like life itself. They were really living in the soul, the someplace else, the dreamland they would one day reach. There was the chorus: *Va pensiero* . . . He hummed along with it, *Fly, my thoughts, on golden wings to the fatherland . . . my beautiful but lost fatherland.* . . . It was in the middle of the chorus that Vinnie came in with Maria's youngest son.

"Turn off that record," Vinnie said to Angelo. Shocked at the sight of his mother, Angelo obeyed, and remained by the phonograph. "Oh, Maria," Vinnie sighed, settling her blanket around her. He sat next to her on the bright green Castro convertible sofa she had bought on sale.

"How did it happen?" Vinnie asked.

"She just felt weak. She called her neighbor and her neighbor called me," Nino said. When he finished telling them how the priest refused her rites and how he and Laura had gone to Our Lady of Perpetual Help, Saint Joseph's, Mount Carmel, and the Church of the Holy Rosary, no one said a word.

"We could keep trying other churches," Angelo said. "I have my car." He had trouble looking at his mother.

"It won't work," Vinnie said. "Once they refuse, they keep refusing. Let's take her home to my place. Mulberry Street isn't Astoria. We can call Father Romano and tell him she died visiting me."

"Tony Romano," Nino said. "I never thought of him. He would understand."

"He'll understand better if you don't explain," Vinnie said. Nino nodded. "But how will we get her out, down all these stairs, without anybody seeing us?"

"We'll need a lookout. Laura, you go down one flight ahead. Motion if it's clear. We'll do it one flight at a time. If someone's going up, we'll rush past and say we're taking her to the hospital. If they're going down ahead of us, we'll just stop and wait. Maybe we'll be lucky and there won't be anybody."

"I don't like this," Angelo said. "Why don't we just call the funeral home or the police or whoever you call. This whole thing is probably illegal anyhow." He was close to tears. "I don't like to see her hauled around like a bag of onions."

"If she was a bag of onions, we wouldn't be taking all this trouble," Laura said, putting her arm around him.

"Angelo," Vinnie encouraged, "this is not the time to think."

Vinnie already had his arm around Maria and was trying to support her head.

"You help with her other side and feet," he told Angelo, moving toward the door.

Nino watched them make it down the first flight of stairs and turned back into the apartment. It was good to have Vinnie around, he thought. It was even right for Maria to go back to the old neighborhood. He switched off the lights and made sure the phonograph was off. If only they could get her safely to Vinnie's it would all work out, he thought, putting the record back in its paper jacket. He took his cane and made his way to the door, pulling it shut behind him, leaving the ginger ale warming in the summer twilight that filtered through the window.

It hadn't been possible to carry Maria down five flights unnoticed, Nino discovered. The heat had brought everybody out. Agnese, Maria's neighbor, even had to be told what was going on. "Maria," she said, "would have loved this. She always did things her way. She never even liked to use the regular garbage. She used to carry her garbage out in a plastic bag and put it in a wire basket the city has on the corner. It was a regular game with the cop on the block. One time he followed her three blocks until she got tired of carrying her garbage around. She waited for him to catch up and handed it to him. When he put it down to write a ticket, she took his pen and said, 'Don't you have anything better to do than bother old ladies?' She was something." She patted Maria and went on ahead of them, just in back of Laura, to divert whomever they met.

In the car, Nino and Laura sat next to Maria. Nino was nervous.

"I hope you appreciate everything we're doing for you," Laura said to Maria.

"She would have done it for you," Vinnie said.

"I won't need to have it done for me," Laura said.

"I hope this works," Nino said. "Tony Romano and I go back a long way, but I haven't seen him since. . . . " He motioned to his legs. His stroke, climax of his diabetes, had left him a limping old man.

"Father Romano is OK," Vinnie reassured him. "You should see some of the people he's buried. He doesn't ask questions. If the Church was only for angels. . . . " He shrugged.

When they reached Vinnie's house, Laura sat in the driver's seat so they wouldn't get a ticket while Angelo and Vinnie helped Maria inside.

"What will I do if a cop asks me to move?" she asked nervously. "I don't even have a driver's license."

"If they see you, they won't ask," Vinnie said, motioning Angelo to take Maria's other side.

When they got Maria into the apartment, they propped her up so she could sit on the convertible sofa in the living room. Adela, Vinnie's wife, put a plaid blanket over Maria's legs and tucked it in, covering the worn green upholstery. She fidgeted with the doily, crocheted by Vinnie's mother, that covered the back of a grass-green armchair.

"Maria always liked to be with people," Adela said, trying to think of something good to say.

"With her family," Nino corrected.

"You're right about that," Laura said, relieved to be out of the car. "She was all for her family. Whatever she was," she said resignedly, sitting on a heavy mahogany side chair, "her place is with us."

"Living or dead?" Angelo asked dryly.

While Vinnie called Father Romano, Adela brought out cold cuts and put them on the large table that filled most of the room. She went back to the kitchen and heated up the lasagna she had made two days before. They sat around the table and nodded that this was probably Maria's last dinner on this side.

"My son, Vinnie Junior, made this himself," said Vinnie, putting a gallon jug on the table. "He has all the equipment and a real touch. It's better than Chianti." He filled water glasses half full and passed them around. "It's also good with Seven-Up, but taste it this way first." He raised his own glass. "I guess we could drink this one for Maria." He held his glass toward her. "May you find your rest," he said genially.

"May you find your rest!" they echoed.

By the time Father Romano showed up they were relaxed and filled with warmth. Nino hobbled to the door as Adela was telling him how glad she was to see him and offering him a glass of wine.

"Nino," Father Romano said, surprised. "You here? It's been a few years now since I've seen you," he said, taking in his gray face and his cane. "When did this happen?" he asked, covering Nino's lameness with a sweep of his hand.

"It's been a while now," Nino said. "I couldn't run for first base today."

Tony Romano shook his head. "We're all getting older," he said. "Who was taken?"

"Maria," Nino said. "It was Maria."

"I remember her very well," Father Romano lied. "She was . . . ," he groped for words, " . . . so full of life."

"In those days we were all full of life. Remember how we would run around the hills in Ventimiglia and hide out in the cemetery?" Nino asked. "Now, one by one, we're going in. Remember the sign over the entrance?"

Father Romano thought for a minute. "It doesn't come back," he said.

"You were thinking of other things then. Then," Nino prodded him with his cane, "you weren't so respectable."

"What did it say?" Father Romano asked.

"It said: 'Remember you who enter me; as we are now so you shall be.' "

Father Romano smiled. "She was a wonderful woman, Maria. All for her children. At least," he continued, stepping toward her chair, "she left among those she loved." He raised his hand in benediction and began, while they all gathered around Maria, "Nomine Patris, Filii, Spiritus Sancti. . . . "

When he left, telling Nino he would come to see him, they all felt suddenly low. They went back to the table, and Adela brought out pastry and coffee while Laura cleared the lasagna dishes.

"Don't you think it's time to call the funeral parlor and have her picked up?" Laura said, sitting down.

"We haven't finished having coffee," Nino told her. "Sit down."

"We don't even have a death certificate," Laura said.

"You don't need a piece of paper to tell you she's gone," Vinnie said. "Around here, Moretti's takes care of everything."

"Laura's right," said Angelo. "I'll call the funeral parlor. They may take a while to come."

"Romano always had a good heart," Nino said. "They don't make priests like that anymore."

"He's OK," Vinnie agreed, "maybe a little too fond of the wine."

"Where's Junior and Adele Ann?" Laura asked.

"He's working on his car and she's out with her boyfriend," Vinnie said, looking at his watch. "Maybe Moretti's will come for Maria before they get home."

"It's better that they don't know what happened," Laura said. "I'll tell Gina Maria died, but nothing else. This business might give them wrong ideas. How can you make them respect religion if they know what you have to go through just to make the Church do the right thing?"

"Well," Vinnie said, "they came through after all. Those Irish twerps aren't the Church. Romano with all his faults understands more."

"You're right," said Laura. "It's people like Maria who always say the wrong thing who need the Church. It was wrong not to pray for her. It's a sin to be like that," she said.

"We'll gain an indulgence for this," Adela said, not content to leave it with an insult to the priest.

"Don't be too sure," Vinnie said. "Didn't they do away with indulgences when they got rid of Saint Christopher?"

"They'll send someone for Mom," Angelo said, coming back from the telephone. "They're not busy tonight."

"And the doctor?" asked Laura.

"They have someone. You were right," he said to Vinnie. "The old neighborhood is different."

"Have another drink," Adela urged. "You look tense. It isn't every day you lose a mother."

"I haven't lost her yet," said Angelo, nodding toward Maria. "She's still here. Alive or dead, her place is with her family, right?" His stomach seemed to beat, contracting and relaxing in a painful rhythm.

"Calm down," Adela advised.

"I'm not tense," Angelo snapped. "I'm not upset! I just wonder why we have to do things this way. The lying, carrying her body around, talking to her as though she were alive. If she were she would have told you she didn't give a damn where she was buried. She didn't care about those things."

"At the end," Nino said, "everyone cares about those things. She would never have found her rest buried in a place far from her family, in ground that had never been blessed."

"Even your father is there," Laura added.

"Yeah," said Vinnie. "Maybe they play the mandolin on the other side too."

"There is no other side," said Angelo. "And if there were, what difference would a prayer make that was said as the result of all this lying? There is no truth in it."

"Truth?" asked Vinnie, irritated.

"What are you talking about?" asked Nino. "You think that Irishman's prayer would have counted more? When I was a boy my mother would tell me how they treated the Italian priests like servants. You think their prayers count more than ours?"

"This is different," Angelo insisted. "This is a deliberate fraud."

"Fraud!" Nino shouted furiously. "It's not your place to worry about whether God feels tricked or not. It's not your worry, it's His. It's your job to make sure your mother is buried in the right place. What happens afterwards is out of your hands. Anyway, God doesn't think in terms like 'fraud.' "

"How do you know how God thinks?" demanded Angelo.

"I don't," Nino admitted. "But it doesn't matter. Look, you're tired. You've been through a lot. Don't worry about what is or isn't true." He softened. "You're a good boy, Angelo, but you're confused. She brought you up to follow the rules, but you were born here and you haven't made up your mind which rules to follow. If you look for rules based on 'truth' and 'feelings' you'll make yourself unhappy because you'll never find a foolproof way of telling which is which. You'll spoil your life worrying over nothing you can solve. I'm Maria's older brother. Your father is dead, you are young. It's my place to bury her correctly even though she shot her mouth off like a woman."

"You think the way you do things is a solution?" Angelo demanded. "You're always arguing for the old ways. You don't just follow them, you hang on to them as though they're all that's saving you from going under. But they don't help. They have no meaning here. Look at Carlino!" Angelo said.

"Your brother is much older than you," Vinnie broke in. "Don't bring him into this."

"In Italy he had to get married," Angelo went on, ignoring him. "The parents of his girl tell him, 'You don't marry Luisa, your bones go to America, not you.' She's sixteen; he's thirty-two. They have nothing in common. But he marries her. They have the baby."

"If there was a baby," Adela said, "they had something in common."

"It was right for her father to make him marry her if he had . . . " Nino made a gesture.

"But what good was it? He was twice her age. Over there, maybe things would work out. But they are here. The child is seven, in school. Luisa learned English and has a good job.

Now she wants a divorce because she doesn't love him. Her parents tell her if she gets a divorce they will never speak to her again. He's afraid she'll leave. If she leaves, he says he'll have nothing. She serves papers on him twice, but she doesn't leave the house."

"That's right," Laura interrupted. "A woman should never be the one to leave the house."

"Let him finish," Nino said.

"So they live together. Nothing goes on between them. They just . . . coexist in the same house. Everyone else in this country gets a divorce. Everyone else dies without being hauled around in search of a priest who doesn't ask questions. But not us. With us, if you were brought up one way, forget it. Your life is set in cement. There's no point in trying to change. Mom would have liked things to be different," Angelo said. "She hated the way we live."

"You're wrong," Nino said. "She didn't hate the way we live. She just wanted to be a little freer." An image of Maria running through the streets of Ventimiglia, up the hill to the cemetery, racing after a pack of urchins, passed through his mind. "She liked to go her own way; for a woman she was something of an anarchist," he mused. "She would get tired of the family, of doing what she was told. But she found," Nino said, warming to his point, "that the ways which made her feel free only led to more and more responsibility."

"What responsibilities?" Angelo demanded. "What are you talking about?"

"You," Nino said. "You and your brothers and sisters. But once she discovered her duty, she did it, no matter what. She was an anarchist at heart," he repeated. "If she could have changed things, she wouldn't have changed them the way you want. You want to be one of them. You want to follow their rules instead of ours. But what are their rules? Premarital sex with contraceptives? Marriage vows you can change your mind about three weeks later? Contracts for everything that show you mistrust everyone you deal with? When we want to change we don't put our trust in other people's rules. We assume the burden. Look at Carlo Tresca! Look at your uncle Sal! Remember your cousin Gesuele!" Nino hoisted himself up on his cane. "That is individualism like Seneca praised— personal responsibility for the good of others. Your mother knew the price of the freedom she wanted. She paid it. Her life is in order. You see?" he demanded, flourishing his cane. "She has come to rest. You look at us and you see we are crude. I know what you think. You think I am a cripple because I can't control my diabetes, my appetite. You think that your mother died with nothing but a few records. I look at us and I see that whatever we are, and no matter what we feel, we do the right thing.

"That young priest was one of you," Nino cried. "He put a stain on his soul just to follow rules. He thinks he's right because he followed the book. You can't absolve yourself by following a book. Romano knows that. You look down on him because he accepts things. He doesn't ask questions because he knows the answers don't matter. What's right doesn't have anything to do with opinions, answers, personal things. There is no middle ground of contracts, sincerity, feelings," he said with disgust. "And the ways you want to follow are even worse than the priest's. Changing this, changing that. Sooner or later you'll see that everything that changes, changes for the worse. You know one of the worst punishments in Dante's hell was to doom a soul to change forever from one thing to another. If Dante were alive today, he would say, 'That soul is a spoiled kid.' " Nino shook his cane.

"Take it easy," Vinnie said. "Every time you let your diploma talk, you don't sound like yourself. Angelo is OK.

He's one of us, aren't you, Angelo," he said soothingly. "It isn't easy to lose a mother like Maria, and he's holding up very well."

"Be careful," Nino said, pointing to Angelo, but winding down, "that you don't let her down by becoming a fool. Don't question whether she should have received the rites or if she should be buried with the likes of us. You are a man. You are supposed to know who you are and what you want."

"He knows, he knows," Vinnie said, "he just wants to be accepted. They all want that."

Angelo sat, seething. He could never figure why, since Nino was so obviously wrong, it was so hard to beat him. His certainty gave him an edge, but that couldn't be all of it. Gina thought he was really attracted to Nino's opinions because Nino made everything make sense. When he talked, Gina said, everything hung together in one piece, like a glued puzzle. Even what didn't fit, didn't fit for reasons you could understand. Things could go wrong, or break down, but that was only a lapse in a system that was totally synchronized. "You'll never get the better of him," Gina had told Angelo, "because you would like things to make sense, too. You don't argue with your whole heart." Angelo had been suspicious that she was putting him down, but she wasn't. "What do you do?" he had demanded roughly, "if you have it figured?"

"Me? I don't do anything at all," she had replied with a smile. "I believe everything he says." He had turned away, disgusted. But he was here doing everything Nino said, and where was she?

"You make me sick," Angelo said to Nino.

"It's a sin to fight in front of your mother," Laura said as the doorbell rang.

"Whether I make you sick or not," Nino said darkly, "answer the door and take your mother to the funeral home."

Angelo got up and walked to the door. He watched as the men from Moretti's put Maria on a stretcher and followed them out without saying goodbye to anyone.

"What makes you sick," Nino called out after him, "is that you can't admit you're one of us."

Angelo slammed the door.

"What a terrible thing for Maria's last dinner to end in a fight like that," said Adela, "when the lasagna was still good."

"It was even better than it was on Sunday," Nino agreed.

"He's just a kid," Vinnie said. "Don't forget, of all Maria's sons, he's the one who helped. The others were glad to leave it to us. You have to go by what he did."

"He may be the best of them," Nino said. "But you can't excuse all of them by saying they're just kids. They're all just kids. Yours, mine, hers," he gestured to where Maria had sat through dinner.

"Sometimes they're all just trouble," Vinnie agreed. "My boy is all right, but he doesn't have as much ambition as he should. Adele Ann is a sweet girl, but she's too pretty for her own good."

Nino nodded. Adele Ann was a beauty. "They're all after her?" he said.

"They're all after her," Vinnie agreed. "It's worse with a girl. What can you do? There's a limit to how much you can watch. The neighborhood boys keep away. I mean, they behave because they're afraid of me. But who knows who else she meets in school. Send a girl to school, you send her into trouble."

"You worry too much about it," Laura said. "My father used to say, what's the good of teaching a girl to write. If they can write, they get in trouble writing love letters! What an attitude! They do things different now than when we were young. It's better. Nino had to take my father along every

time we went to a movie. And I . . . "—she hesitated to admit—"was twenty-seven. Remember, Nino?"

"How could I forget?" Nino said sourly. "We were engaged for nine years."

"My father was afraid my sister would go to a dance one night when my mother was in the hospital and he had to visit her. So he actually tied her to the bed to stop her from going. That is insane. It's good for them to go out and know each other. Then maybe they won't make the mistakes we did."

"You aren't saying we made mistakes," Adela prodded.

"No, no. I mean people of our time. In the olden days," Laura said hastily.

"You say that because you don't have to worry about Gina. Not that she isn't pretty. But she isn't interested in boys," Adela added quickly.

Nino looked at Adela. Gina was pretty, but she wasn't Adele Ann. Adele Ann looked like the young Ava Gardner, only more voluptuous.

"Who knows what Gina's interested in," Nino said. "She doesn't go out, not that much, but she gets phone calls all the time."

"What can happen on the telephone?" Laura asked.

Nino looked at her. She was exasperating. "She's secretive and deep," he said. "She's deep. You never know what she thinks. And she's fresh. If you tell her she's too secretive, she says, 'Didn't you teach me not to talk too much? Didn't you always say,'" Nino mimicked, "'Chi gioca solo non perde mai'? The man who plays alone never loses."

"That," Vinnie said, "applies to men. A man has to keep his mouth shut to get on in the world. When a woman isn't talking it means she has something to hide."

Nino nodded. Adela stared at Vinnie. Laura stared at her cannoli.

"The way I see it," Vinnie continued seriously, "I think she's that way because you let her have her own room. It isn't good for a girl to have that. She could sleep in the living room, like Adele Ann. Otherwise they get used to privacy. Too much privacy is no good for a girl. It spoils them."

"She has too many ideas of her own," Nino agreed. "She thinks things will be possible that won't be possible. She wants to go to college, so what does she do when I say yes? She listens to a teacher who tells her to apply to a fancy women's college. I can tell her in advance she won't get in. What do places like that want with Sicilian girls from Astoria? When the letter comes rejecting her, I open it and take it to high school so she would have to read it in front of the class. When she saw me, she thought I was bringing good news. She couldn't imagine I would take the trouble with my leg to bring her a rejection. I figured she'll start to cry, feel humiliated, and it will be all over. Instead she reads the letter, doesn't flinch, and says to me, 'You know bad news can always wait.' She just shrugs to her friends. Now she's more determined. This one," he shrugged, pointing to Laura, "only eggs her on."

"What's wrong if she goes to college?" Laura demanded, barely able to contain herself. "Do you think I brought her up so she could be tied to a chair, or sleep in a living room? She could be an elementary school teacher. That's a good job for a woman. What's wrong with that?"

"Nothing if that's all she'll learn. But that isn't what she wants," Nino said with a mildness that should have made Laura suspicious.

"What do you think she wants?" Laura asked.

"She wants," Nino said comfortably, "to get away from me. Just like Angelo," he said. "She wants to be one of them. But she can't be." He began to nibble his sfogliatelli again.

"She won't be one of them?" Laura demanded angrily. "Why not? You think she's not good enough?"

"No," Nino said, "that has nothing to do with it. She'll never feel she belongs the way she does with us."

"She doesn't feel she belongs with us," Laura protested.

"But she does," Nino said with finality.

"Maybe you've been trying the wrong approach," Vinnie suggested. "You can catch more flies with honey than vinegar. Tell her since your stroke you can't afford to let her go; you need the money from her working."

"She is working," Nino admitted. "She has a full-time summer job at Columbia."

"She's willing to work her way through?" Vinnie asked.

Nino nodded.

"Then what can you do." Vinnie shrugged. "You should be glad she's ambitious. Why don't you encourage her? If you set yourself against this, it will only make trouble. See how it goes first."

"That's it, Vinnie," Laura said. "Why should they live like us?"

"What's wrong with the way we live?" Nino asked. "My father used to say, 'When you leave the old ways, you know what you will lose, but not what you will find.' That's a Sicilian proverb."

"Remember the Neapolitan proverb, 'When there's no money coming in the door, love flies out the window'?" Laura demanded.

"What has that got to do with anything?" Nino said.

"Everything. I mean, not the money, but the way of living. When we had a chance to buy a house, you wouldn't do it. You would rather live in a tenement. We don't even know anyone who lives in an elevator building. You're the only person I ever heard say good things about the Depression,"

Laura said in disgust. "Where did your education get you?"

"People were nicer in the Depression," Nino said. "Less pretentious."

Laura went on furiously. "You're happy if you can take a train to Yankee Stadium and eat hot dogs. In the meantime you brood about everybody who wants to do something else. You think everyone will fail or go wrong before they even try." She stuck her thumb angrily in Vinnie's ashtray and rubbed ashes onto it. "You want to mourn?" she said harshly. "Here," she yelled, rubbing her thumb on his forehead. "You can have Ash Wednesday early this year!"

"Laura!" Adela said, shocked. "Calm down."

"He doesn't mourn for his sister because she's dead. He drinks wine to his sister. But he mourns for my daughter because she's alive!" Laura said angrily.

"She secretive, she's deep, and you encourage her," Nino said quietly. "Put on your sweater."

"We've all been through a lot," Vinnie said. "We all worry about the kids. Let's just forget this. It was good that we could have a drink with Maria at the end."

"May she rest in peace," Laura murmured, shocked at what she had done.

"May she rest in peace," Adela agreed.

When Laura and Nino reached the street, Laura said, "I shouldn't have gotten so upset in front of them."

"No," Nino agreed, "you shouldn't have."

"You shouldn't have said those things about Gina in public," Laura persisted.

When will she learn to shut up? Nino thought to himself. This one won't keep quiet and the other one won't talk. The BMT rumbled; the car, covered with graffiti, careened rheumatically from side to side. He closed his eyes, gathering peace from the steady noise that drowned out all other sounds. Tony Romano was free, he thought. No wife, no

daughter. No wonder he looked so young. Nino shook his
head and sat silently, his hands resting on his cane, all the
way to their stop.

When they reached home Nino unlocked the door, held it
open, and watched Laura walk into the apartment. They had
no foyer, but instead a hall twenty feet long and thirty inches
wide with a humped floor curving over a water pipe that had
been laid beneath it. On either side of the wall hung family
photographs, images that seemed to fall away from Nino as
he limped past them. In the dim light, the eyes of the living
and the dead seemed to stare at each other like adversaries
poised on opposite sides of the hall. Faces from the past, they
were locked in their separate frames, confronting each other,
never together. There was nothing but memory to press
them into a whole, into one family portrait. And no one but
Nino seemed to want that. The ashes Laura had pressed
upon him seemed to have fallen between him and Vinnie,
dividing even them. Vinnie would think less of him because
she did it.

"Make me some coffee," Nino called out.

Laura gave no reply, but in the white kitchen where the
walls glared under a round flourescent light, she reached for
the coffee pot still on the range.

Nino watched her from the doorway, his face gray and
grim. He opened the cabinet where Laura kept the dishes
they used every day. He took out a dinner plate and threw
it to the floor. Then he threw another and another until the
linoleum was strewn with bits of flower-patterned crockery
and shards of glass seemed to have gone everywhere.

"You think you can criticize me in front of my nephew and
get away with it! You think you can humiliate me with ashes!"
Nino demanded.

Laura stood silently, watching him.

"Never do that again! If a wife can't say anything positive

about her husband, she shouldn't say anything at all. You insult my dead sister, you encourage my daughter to rebel. You had better start behaving like my wife!" Nino's voice, full and low in its rage, hardened. "You've gone too far. You and Gina have gotten out of hand. It's going to stop! Do you understand?"

Laura nodded. She had pushed him too far. He wouldn't listen to her until he calmed down. She waited for his anger to pass.

Nino could see that she was humoring him. Whenever she behaved sensibly and didn't say anything to make more trouble it turned out to be a ploy, he thought. He picked up a coffee cup and threw it on the floor.

"Now clean up this mess," he said quietly, turning away. He went into the living room and sat down in his favorite chair. It was up to him to clean up the mess she had made of Gina. His body ached from the long day and the effort of doing right by Maria. His loss of her inflamed the painful memories of all that had ever eluded him. It was terrible how everything was falling apart. Where was the order, the wholeness of life? The dead became dust, but the living too seemed to fall from his fingers, blown here and there by the will to escape and outrage the obligations they had to each other.

Nino could hear Laura angrily slamming what was left of the dishes into the metal garbage pail. The smell of coffee was beginning to fill the apartment. Nino smiled wearily. How like her to be furious at him while she made him coffee at the same time. She could never escape his reach and yet she had let their daughter grow slippery and elusive. A dark apprehension of what it might take to bring Gina back in line overtook him. But Gina, he resolved, tightening his grip on the arm of his chair, would not get away.

Two

"Pops," said the fruit man, "your daughter passed by at three-thirty. She was carrying a load of books for over there," he added, nodding toward the library.

"Thanks," said Nino, limping into the fruit store. "How are the tangerines today?" He tore open the spicy skin to sample it himself. "Give me five," he said, assessing the tart juice. It was good to be in a neighborhood where everybody knew you. He had been here for forty-two years now. He knew every empty lot, garage, playground. When he was still a youth worker he would ferret his kids out from under cars where they were trying to stash drugs, from playgrounds where they played basketball and drank beer instead of going to school. Now they were in their thirties, some of them. He'd meet them on the street, walking their kids. They would show them off; they would tell him he straightened them out. They would try not to look surprised at how white-eyed and crippled he had become. They were good kids at heart, Nino thought. Stealing cars, robbing phone booths—it was what you could expect. It was different with his last boy, the fifth-grader who had set fire to P.S. 5 just to see the panic-stricken rush for safety, wondering how many kindergarteners would be trampled.

He tucked the bag of tangerines under his arm, turned the corner, sat heavily on a bench, and waited. Here everything was in order. He could see the library two blocks away, the playground across the street where mothers pushed babies in little swings at one end and old men played bocce at the other. Some of the old men had dug up the grass and planted tomatoes. Johnny, the old carpenter, had built an arbor with latticework across the top. The grapevines nearly covered it now. It would be cool and sweet in there, Nino thought appreciatively. He kept his back to the space where P.S. 5 had been. Six stories of old red brick surrounded by a cement yard, the school had filled the middle of the block. How many teenagers he had retrieved from the monkey bars where they sat smoking pot on summer nights! It was all gone. All the rubble had been cleared away and only a swept, fenced-in emptiness was left. Somehow it was ominous, that space where nothing happened now.

Still, why couldn't Laura like it around here anymore? He knew she had been disappointed when he had refused to take the house by the river. But buying it would have meant borrowing from her father and living with him. How could he when the old man was so rigidly set in his ways? Laura had wanted to live near the river, on the sweet street, the winding block of private houses with yards filled with rose-bushes and fig trees. The masons and construction people who had made money all lived there, some in houses fantastic with stone grottoes to the Blessed Virgin, with cement animals coyly wide-eyed, with stone doghouses that looked like monuments to a dead emperor. Winding down to the river, toward the field where young men played soccer, the street ended in Astoria Park, where the park met the shore. The river beach, stippled with rocks and pebbles, invited all the kids to send pebbles soaring over the water, plopping in a finale of spreading circles. Across the river stood the skyline of Manhattan, rippling shadows over the oily water, the late-afternoon sun turning the river-city into a mirage of power and defiance. Unreal beyond the fig trees and little rosebush gardens, Manhattan was always there, a foreign country with different ways. In the park, huge stone columns that supported the Triboro Bridge had been fenced off so nobody could climb them; the arching steel and cement curving up against the immense weight of the roadway soared toward the city and beyond. If it seemed like a route to possibility, it also implied that some possibilities were out of reach.

Nino was so absorbed he almost failed to notice Gina walking down the library steps. She was all dressed up, he noticed sourly, and she carried a paper bag. Nobody dresses like that for a library. The city, he thought. She must be going to the city dressed like that. He moved as quickly as he could to the El, crossing the street so he could climb the stairway she wouldn't take. The green banister, warm under his hand, helped prop him up step by step as he hurried to the top. He had to get there before she saw him. He hobbled out of the stairwell just in time to see through the grimy window that she had reached the opposite stairway. Right again!

Dropping his token in, Nino moved to the shadowy end of the platform, past the token seller in the throne room they had built for coin changers years before. Now the fancy cupola seemed feathered, peeling and fluttering huge green paint chips like a molting bird in the stale air. Nino settled into the shadows of the platform and opened his newspaper in front of his face. No matter that it wasn't today's. The thing was to have one folded in your pocket all the time, just in case. She always goes to the other end of the platform to see over the dome of Saint Demetrios's church. But the train was already rumbling behind him. She reached the platform and sprinted, so intent on making it she didn't see him limping into the third car. He moved to the second car while the train was in the tunnel. He could see her through the glass windows in the doors between the cars. She had stood up, waiting for the train to stop at Fifty-ninth Street. She can't wait to get out, he thought. Is she just going to Bloomingdale's? He pushed the question away because Bloomingdale's wouldn't make her look that eager. And what was she carrying in that bag? My bag! he remembered suddenly. He must have left it on the bench.

She had been so eager to make the train that it had taken Gina a minute after sitting down to realize that she had glimpsed Nino limping into another car. What can he want in the city? she wondered. Me! it came to her. He is following me. Had he done it before? It was shocking, sickening; his hobbled pursuit of her radiated mistrust, contempt for her privacy; it showed how low he must have held her to think it was necessary. She began to feel dizzy and hot with rage. Even the spectacular view of the city she always waited for, as the curving rails peaked before the train descended into the tunnel, couldn't dispel her shock. She rose, moving to the door, staring out the window as the train fled underground.

For a long time now, she could see that she was everything to him, that he could only deal with losing her by controlling her life, so that whatever happened to her would show his mark. You don't have to do this, Nino, she whispered to the shut door. How could it have come to this? He had always been so kind—wonderful, really—when she was little. The trips to the park, the circus, the patience he had playing catch with her, the hours of talk, talk, talk, the trips to the Statue of Liberty, his rhapsodic, crazy feeling for city streets—there had been a lot between them. And then there came his somber and suspicious looks, his careful observations of her at weddings, in the neighborhood, until he seemed to be all eye. Totally vigilant, he watched what she ate, what she left, what she read. Why had it happened? What had she done? The subway hurtled noisily through the tunnel, lurching from side to side, throwing her against the door.

Had she been thirteen, fourteen? It was already hard to place the moment he began to turn away from her. He had encouraged her to be strong, tough, independent, unafraid of getting hurt, and then he betrayed it all. His stroke only seemed to have intensified his need to close in. He had had an easy time at first, forcing her into a confused silence. She had withdrawn into her room, turning it into half refuge, half escape, so that it looked like nothing else in the tiny, dim apartment. It was dark, facing an alley; sun never shone into it, not even as a reflection bouncing off the windows of the building that loomed behind the alley wall. She knew every crack, every fissure, every gradation of gray in that wall.

She had painted her room a warm ivory. She had picked out a low bookcase, a corner piece, and two end pieces in unfinished pine; the whole unit looked built-in. The space of thirty inches that was left between the bookcase and her closet had a small teak desk she had placed at right angles to the wall. Over the desk was a print of Modigliani's *Seated Girl* in warm flesh tones with rusts and browns and golds. Opposite the bookshelves was a bed. She had thrown out the ruffled bedspread Laura had bought her, and fitted it out as a daybed with pillows in rust, gold, and ivory. In front of it, against the wall between the bed and the door to the room, was an old dresser with a huge mirror over it. Next to it, on a hook near the door, hung a fishnet drawstring bag that held a Speedo bathing suit and cap. The dresser top was messy with eyeliners, eye shadows, lipsticks, glosses, and blushers, which Nino referred to as junk. Nino had tolerated it all, even the hours spent hunched before the mirror, staring alternately at *Vogue* and at her face, following directions for achieving special effects.

"What are you doing," Nino would ask, half joking, from the doorway. "Putting on makeup or a Halloween mask? Who are you trying to be?" He would pick up the magazine and browse through. "You look better than this, anyway," he would say pleasantly. "This one looks like she hasn't eaten for months, a famine victim who got mugged. Look at the bruises around her eyes." He would point to the carefully darkened lids. "Is this the style? Just make sure you wash it off before you go out," he would say, walking off. "Makeup is ridiculous on a girl your age."

He had treated her like a kid dressing up in her mother's clothes. Except that Laura never wore makeup, nothing but lipstick. It was, she guessed, part of trying on other lives, other faces, faces that said different things, made whatever sexual statements can be made with blue eyelids, or smoky sinuous lines that widened the eyes and made them seem almond-shaped, oriental, exotic.

He had had a sense of humor about it all. Next to the back issues of *Mademoiselle*, *Glamour*, and *Vogue*, she kept stacks of used paperbacks. "Do you buy these by the pound?" he had joked, picking up and replacing one after the other. He saw that she had made a special place for the books he had given her. She had kept them well, he thought. A good thing, the reading habit. And what trouble could she get into, alone in her room?

She had watched him turn over everything on her shelves with such deepening concern that she came to regard every attempt to come into her room as a kind of trespass. The books, the makeup, and the reading were all part of something she suspected he hadn't grasped. Nino, you idiot, she thought, watching him quizzically thumbing through her things, you don't get it at all. It's all the same thing, all part of the trip out. She had found escapes in the other lives she read about, lives that gave full weight to the fear and joy she felt, the quick plunges from elation to depression. There was truth in their violence, their rebellion, the long praise of adventure, the belief that everything could be survived, the thirst for life at the edge. Even the books he had given her, even the *Odyssey* had it. True, the adventures were less spectacular after that.

But the aversion to boredom was always there. It was there in the latest stories of men on the run from age, pregnant wives, and responsibility. Nino would probably have nothing but contempt for these men. But she had always agreed with them. Look what a deadening misery it was, this business of family ties, wives, children, hanging on to your neck. Laura had been a wonderful wife and mother, and where had it gotten her? She encouraged Gina to go to school as much as she did to get married. It was clear she didn't want Gina to follow in her footsteps. Who wouldn't want to feel that life could be all highs with nothing to drag you down? It had never occurred to her that the infatuations with freedom she had read about were celebrations of maleness until she began to pay attention to Nino's conversations with Vinnie, until the two of them made it clear she wasn't welcome, until it was unmistakable that they saw the crucial thing about her was her sex.

It was one thing to recognize that there was a double standard, that men were different, but it was quite another to know what to do about it. It went beyond the practical. Most of the women she had known had always worked. Laura had worked and worked; the sight of her in the steaming shop, hunched over a sewing machine, never failed to make Gina's heart sink. She didn't make a lot, but she had her own money, and she had an independent mind, even if she didn't show much of it to Nino. She showed it to me, Gina thought, in all the times she had made clear she wanted me to live a different kind of life. Laura and her covert rebellion. She had run the house, done the cooking and laundry, raised her, and worked besides. Nino never lent a hand. He had Laura's number and wouldn't give an inch. That was the way it seemed to be: people who had privileges weren't about to give them up just because they were unfair. It was easier to find excuses for the way things were. Maybe there were men who were different, but Nino—who was, after all, no fool— didn't think so. His one sexual lesson to her was simple and succinct: Never trust a man.

It was a problem. Poor Nino. He had put himself in a terrible spot, she was beginning to realize. He liked women, but didn't respect them because he thought they were spineless, easily swayed, subject to force. He had wanted her as an ally, an alter ego. She smiled grimly. So, Nino, you got one. Your lectures on perseverance, beginning when I was four (you called it stick-to-it-iveness), your determination to make me take any humiliation or trouble you dished out without flinching—you had called it building character. It paid off, Nino, she whispered to the shut door, you succeeded. Now I'm not afraid of anything you can dish out. She winced at her own words. It was a pep talk, but still there was truth in it.

There was no exit from this. Already his watchfulness had narrowed her life. She had spent too much time avoiding open fights, forced into the covert way Laura dealt with him. Already she could see she might fall into a passive inwardness, drifting along, numbing herself and not taking charge of her

life, not making a stand. There had been too many escape
fantasies and no escape.

The train seemed to be going incredibly fast, veering from
side to side, its lurching force knocking her around without
her noticing it. She was through escaping into books, into
her obsessions with diets, makeup, dates with boys Nino had
raked over. Things had to be different now. Alex was so
much sharper, so much more sophisticated than anyone she
had ever known. So far she had kept him from knowing all
the bad parts. It was true he was as much of a guru as Nino,
but at least, she thought, what he wants to teach me, I want
to know. I picked this one myself.

Now Nino was throwing his shadow across what she wanted.
He was dimming everything. She knew there was something
in her that Nino wanted; he wouldn't let up until he got it.
As though he had given her a gift and was trying to steal it
back. What was it? It had to do with the radiance she felt,
the discovery of another way of feeling, of an elation that
grew in her like a longed-for child. She could sense it had a
purpose, this mood, a meaning, but she couldn't yet say what
it was. If Nino killed it now, there might not be another, not
one that glowed with so much promise. Give it up, Nino, she
murmured. You don't have to do this. But she knew that it
was useless to hope.

It worked both ways. Nino can follow, but I can hide. It's
vulgar to hide, she thought. No, it isn't. It's just the price you
have to pay for being alive around him. If he can lie to fix
up Maria's death, I can lie to fix up my life. He wouldn't
follow me if he really knew anything. It's up to me, Nino, to
make sure you never find out anything at all. You always
said, "You have to protect what you have!"

The train lurched to a stop at Fifty-ninth and Lexington.
Nino got out behind her, at first cautious, then less so because

she never looked back. He could see her smiling as she reached the top of the stairs to the street. He hung back. How could she climb so fast? From the top of the stairs he saw her through a small mob of people clustered near the entrance to the train. A young man with a yellow beard had his arm around her. She had given him the bag. He was smiling into it. He hugged her. By the time Nino decided to confront them, they had begun to walk off together. How quickly they walked! His filmy eyes raked over the crowd on Third Avenue. But they were gone.

He shuffled a block in each direction, hoping to glimpse them. Exhausted, he leaned against Bloomingdale's window. Mannequins in shorts, in dresses with plunging necklines and bare backs, stood behind him with legs raised like the Rockettes. The smell of exhaust fumes fulminating in the heat suddenly hit him.

When boys got into trouble, they had problems you could understand. With girls it was always the same thing. But not my daughter, he thought, gripping his cane and beating it against the sidewalk. A creep with a beard. A yellow beard. It was so hard to believe. He heaved himself onto his cane, unable to stop looking. But there were so many people, so many movies. They could have gone anywhere. The possibilities were dizzying; some of them made him gasp. The fumes and heat seared his throat. So he let himself drift with the crowds, dropping from the blistering sun into the subway darkness.

They hadn't gone anywhere near the places Nino searched. They had wandered for a mile until it became clear where they wanted to go.

"What a cave," Gina said when they got there. "You live in a white cave," she repeated, pulling a cushion under her head to see better. The walls were freshly painted white over plaster that had been laid on so lumpily it looked like painted rock, something miraculously hacked out of a mountain on Avenue D and Third Street. There was a door facing her, bolted shut, a heavy metal door not well concealed by the streaked paint that covered it. On either side shelves had been hung on which books stood, neatly arranged in alphabetical order. On the right was a closet with a white sheet attached to a curtain rod as a door. It held a blazer, a poplin jacket, a heavy woolen suit, and three pairs of white jeans, hung like expensive slacks. On the left wall was the entrance, and right next to it, a white metal shower stall and a door leading to a toilet. To reach the apartment, they had walked through the entrance to one tenement and out the back door to an alley where still another building had been placed. To get to Avenue D you had to go through another alley and tenement. He lives in a tenement sandwich, she thought, watching him.

Alex was talking, pacing around looking for something, but she couldn't concentrate enough to hear what he was saying. His body, in the rays of late sunlight that came through the small high window, glowed. He was covered with reddish gold hair. It made him gleam; it felt rough or velvety, depending on where you touched. His thick golden hair and beard, trimmed and clipped with obvious care, shone so that his face seemed lit up. The muscles of his stomach and hips formed an amazing, curving U. After weeks of talking, walking, embracing in the park, nothing about him should seem strange. But the silence of his place after the raucous street, and his beauty, seemed like a tremendous surprise. They had both been giddy since they came in, shedding their clothes for a shower. They had never been alone like this before, and the solitude, after coffee shops and walks down crowded streets, was shocking. He had become remote after being so passionate in doorways. But the day seemed to stretch out far enough to encompass everything. He had chosen a cassette and put it in the tape deck. The music seemed to relax him.

Alex crawled into bed with her, pulling the sheet over them and pressing his face into her breasts. She touched his face, tracing the line between his cheek and beard. He murmured, "Are you disappointed that I didn't jump on you in the shower?"

"What a question," she said. But she didn't really know the answer. "It's so strange, just to be alone with you. I feel as though I don't know you." She reached back under the pillow. "That's so lovely," she breathed.

"You like the tape," he said approvingly.

"I meant the way you feel."

"You have," he began gravely, "a way of saying what you know I want to hear in a way that also makes fun of me." He took her wrists and suddenly pinned each hand to the bed, climbing on top of her. "Don't you know you shouldn't make fun of me," he said.

"I'm not . . . " she began to protest, not sure if he was kidding or not.

He began licking her face, her eyes, her neck. At first she laughed, then she thought it was unpleasant, then she began to dream into it, waiting for what would come next. He stretched her arms, pulling her hands up under the pillows and leaving them there while his body pinned her back. On the smooth sheet under the pillow, there was something hard. Her fingertips reached it and closed around it automatically. It was a piece of metal, a solid pipe, a crowbar. She twisted under him as sharply as she could, forcing him to roll off as she stood and moved away from the bed. She was still holding the crowbar. "What's this?" she said.

Alex looked at her. "Are you going to attack me?" he said, amused.

"What's it doing under your pillow?" she asked, feeling disconcerted by his amusement.

"You trust me, I think," he said. "But you're not really sure what I am or what I'll do next. Is that right?"

She nodded. "Maybe."

"Forget it," he said. "It can be rough down here. I keep it handy, in case someone breaks in. If I'd known we were coming here I would have taken it away this morning."

Gina threw the bar into the corner and sat next to him. His kiss was tender and searching, his tongue somehow able to stir her hunger. She folded herself around him, luxuriating in his skin, his weight, his feel. Suddenly he was gone; he straddled her, bending down to kiss her.

"Come back," she whispered. "Please."

"Not yet." He smiled. "You'll have to wait for what you want."

He looked at her for long moments and then, embracing her until she felt she glowed, rocked her into orgasm. He moaned as he came, curling down on her.

"You are not a virgin," he said quietly. "I was so careful with you. I thought you were."

Excuses, explanations didn't come up easily through the dreaminess, the utter fullness of her mood. An accident with her cousin's bike? A bumpy horse on a merry-go-round? What kind of question was that to ask, anyway?

"No," she said, "I'm not." What possible difference could that make? She was tired of lying.

"There is an old French romance about a man who goes looking for a virgin. He searches all through Rouen, beginning with girls of fifteen, and he works on down until, to find one, he has to try five-year-olds."

"Very touching," she said. "Also very disgusting."

"Let's have supper," he said, getting up. He walked to the refrigerator and took some Polish ham from the center shelf.

He put up water to boil for tea. She watched him from the bed. He was irritated and grumpy. He was, she realized, very complicated. Why had he tried so hard to please her just to spoil it? The question proclaimed itself like a billboard somewhere outside her. She floated above his irritation. There are some gifts, she thought, that you can't take back.

"There's a roach in the sugar," Alex said moodily, peering into the box. "I guess I'll have to get another box. There's a store across the street. I'll be right back." He pulled on his slacks and sandals.

While he was gone she dressed and wandered around the room. She switched the tape off, watching the lights flicker as the system stopped. She was looking idly at the bolted door, wondering where it led, when the telephone rang. Without thinking, she answered it.

"Hello, Alex? Is Alex there?" a woman asked.

"No," Gina said, "he isn't."

"Just tell him Ronnie called," the woman said.

"Will you leave your number?" Gina asked stiffly.

"675-7462," she said, hanging up.

Gina checked the telephone. The number was the same. Maybe it was just a mistake; the woman was surprised to hear her answer.

Coming through the doorway, Alex motioned to the shower. "See . . . we can talk while you drink your tea."

"Very sociable shower," Gina said. Somehow it was hard to talk. He had complained about her silences, and that made them last longer.

"Someone called while you were out. Ronnie. When I asked for her number, she left yours."

"She just moved out," Alex said casually.

"How soon is 'just'?"

"Last week," he said.

"Oh," said Gina, taking it in. So that's how all those romantic walks with me ended.

"But as soon as she left I became innocent as a baby again." He sliced some ham and dropped it on her plate.

"Here's to Baby Alex," she said, raising her iced tea.

He took her in appreciatively. "Look, I felt bruised before, but it's OK now." He reached across the table and touched her face. "I want you to meet my friends. I want you to meet my father. He's fantastic. He'd love you."

The question, she thought, is whether you do. "Where do your parents live?" she asked instead.

"In Philadelphia," Alex said, chewing on his ham and rye.

"I'd love to meet them both, " Gina said insincerely, relieved they weren't in New York. What can you say to any of them? She realized that for all the weeks they had known each other, neither had said much about parents. The less said, the better. Anyway, they all seemed so remote. Everything seemed remote except the whitewashed room, and Alex with his rich hair and hazel-green eyes.

When she got home, she was relieved that everyone had gone to sleep. She could hardly wait to turn out the light and get into bed. As soon as the room was dark, she could smile. She stayed awake just to keep the happiness alive. When she fell asleep, men came running after her in black coats and dark pointed hats. There were six of them, carrying a coffin and running through a park. It was very cold: winter bitterness without snow, the ground frozen brown and bare trees sprinkled here and there with rotting leaves. The men were running toward her. She realized the coffin was for her. She began to run and reached a place like a formal garden, desolate now and out of bloom. In the center was a huge rectangular reflecting pool, still filled and apparently bottomless. The men were reaching her. They set down the coffin on the flagstone walk around the pool and advanced. She had nowhere to turn. She dove into the pool and swam down. At the bottom of the pool it was summer. The water was warm and slightly perfumed; somehow she could breathe in it. There was a sunny cave filled with multicolored fish. I can stay here forever, she thought. But she swam to the surface, and when she did, the park was transformed. It was tropical, filled with heavy, lush foliage. Lily pads floated on the surface with perfect flowers. She touched one and found she could climb on it like a raft. When she did, she realized that she had become half fish.

I got off easy this time, Gina thought, waking up disconcerted but happy. There had been too many dreams lately. She couldn't remember ever dreaming before she had met Alex. But this one was good; maybe it was even an omen. It was 4:30 A.M. She picked up a book and began to read. She liked the time before dawn—between work and Alex she hadn't much time to herself.

It was six o'clock when Laura knocked softly at the door.

"I saw your light," Laura said, coming in with a glass of juice. "You'll ruin your eyes with so much reading."

"I wanted to finish this. I have to return it tomorrow," Gina said guiltily. Half the books she returned were returned unread. Going to the library had become such a convenient lie.

"How are things at work?" Gina asked, wanting to shift the subject away from herself. She hated to lie, so it was better not to talk.

"More of the same," Laura said. "We're making blouses out of such cheap material it unravels while you work. There's so much detail—with tucks and darts and smocking." She waved her hand. "They'll sell them for forty dollars, but they're not worth five with that material. And then," Laura went on, "the girls all have problems. Concetta's daughter had a boy. Poor thing. She was so pretty, too. She ruined her life marrying that boy without a job or even a trade. She was so pretty."

"Yes," Gina said. "She was." She could still remember her coming into high school, hugely pregnant, to sign some papers. She had been crying. "She should have just gone away and given the baby up for adoption, instead of getting married."

"You can't give away a child. Once you have it, that's it. But it's true it's not always like that. In the old neighborhood there was a woman named Anna who was a midwife. She used to do abortions too. She was always busy with one or the other. But Marty, her husband, he did nothing but fool around when she was out. To make a long story short, he put a woman in the family way. When I was your age, I heard Anna tell this story to my mother. She said, 'I didn't want to lose him,' over and over. The woman was single and she thought Marty would marry her because of the baby. So Anna offered the woman an abortion. But the woman thought she was jealous and she wouldn't trust Anna. So Anna reasons with her. She says, 'Look, he's no good. He's supposed to watch the children when he's not working, but instead he lets them run wild and runs around with you. He isn't going to marry you. Do yourself a favor. I'm fifty-eight and I can't do any better. But you are young and pretty and you should learn from your mistakes. So do yourself a favor and get yourself out of the mess you got into.'

"By the time the woman made up her mind, it was too late for an abortion. So Anna offered to take care of her at the end, deliver the baby, give her a few hundred dollars afterward, and keep the child to raise as her own. When the time came for the woman to deliver, she took her into the house and kept her there ten days after the child was born. Then the woman went away. Today that boy is married and lives in California and he never knew Anna wasn't his mother." Laura was visibly impressed.

"Wasn't fifty-eight too old for Anna to pass off a child as her own?" Gina asked, also impressed.

"If Anna had been bothered by questions like that, she could never have pulled it off. It never pays to be too sensitive about what people say."

"She must have been pretty thick-skinned," Gina said, thinking of Marty living with Anna and the pregnant woman.

"Oh, she was. There wasn't much she didn't see or go through. It worked, too, what she did. Marty stayed with her, although he was never much good for anything. But she knew that," Laura mused. "Now you. If you would go out instead of burying yourself in the library every night. If you would only go out with Arthur. He keeps asking you. He's a really good boy. Take my advice. It's not for nothing I'm old enough to be your mother. Arthur is good. He goes to college, he works in the fruit store after school. He's loyal. He would make a good husband. He gives every penny he makes to his mother. How a boy treats his mother, is how he'll treat his wife."

"I'm too young to get married," Gina dodged. "Anyway, Arthur hasn't asked me."

"If you would go out with him, he would ask you," Laura persisted. "He is an exception. Like your father."

"I hope not," Gina said.

"You can say what you like about your father, but he's all for his family. Now Arthur would be exactly like that, only not so Sicilian. If Anna could keep Marty until the age of ninety-four, you can get Arthur to marry you."

"I'm not interested. He's boring and fat."

"Just think about it. A man who isn't handsome makes a better husband because he's grateful to you for marrying him. He appreciates you more," Laura said, getting up.

She has a proverb for every situation, Gina thought, amused. Not to mention a story, an anecdote, a relative who had experienced firsthand everything from a visitation by Saint Teresa to a potato cure for warts. Crazy schemes, bizarre situations erupting in orderly lives—all reminders that since anything could happen, it was better that nothing did. So a boring husband was a hedge against catastrophe—a gambler, a drinker, a womanizer. Having "character" was having the stamina not to be bored or desperate, the stamina to be grateful.

Nino placed a low estimate on unhappiness, even though the impulse to self-pity ran high in him. He was given to sulking depressions from which anything could erupt. "Look at him!" Aunt Anna-Maria would say, qualified for some expertise in despair by her months as a patient at Creedmoor. "What's he got to be unhappy about? Everybody gets old and sick. He gets around. He's happy as a clam in the water," she would certify, licking custard from her fingers.

But Gina knew he wasn't happy. She could see in Laura a stream of small satisfactions, a gift for finding amusement and meaning in daily things, that gave her a steady joyousness. Nino brooded. He brooded out loud because everything he believed in was unraveling. But he was most unhappy be-cause—Gina hesitated for a moment—because of me. I am, she thought, amused, the thorn in his side, the nail through his hand. . . . So we should be quits, because he is that to me. But it wasn't working out that way. There were no arbitrated settlements, no agreements to disagree. There was only guerrilla warfare on both sides, with Nino having the edge. No fair, she thought dreamily, drifting from the kitchen Laura had cleaned. Least fair to Laura, she thought, browsing through her closet, looking for the right dress.

When he heard the door close a second time, Nino stretched and sat up. He wasn't ready to talk to her yet. He wasn't ready to say anything directly. All in good time, he thought. He knew she must have met him at work. Some bum who hung around Columbia. He was sure. Well, he would pay a surprise visit and meet her for lunch. He would watch to see whom she was trying to walk out with and force her to introduce him. One way or another, he would find out his name.

The way things were done today was ridiculous. When Nino had gone out with Laura, the old man went with them. Whenever they went to a movie, he came along. If they went to a dance, he had to take her two sisters, too. They were never alone. When he had to go out and the young one wanted to go somewhere, her father tied her to a chair. He overdid it, Nino admitted to himself. He overdid it. But it was better than doing nothing. Laura thought Gina had good judgment. Good judgment! The words felt like worms in his mouth. She had no judgment. A creep with a beard.

By the time he got to the bursar's office where she worked, it was 11:45. As soon as he walked through the doorway, he saw the jerk working a paper-cutting machine. I knew it, Nino thought grimly. Not for nothing have I tracked people for years.

"Excuse me, young man," Nino said to him politely. "Is this the registrar's office?"

"No," answered Alex, "this is the bursar. The registrar is three doors down, on the right."

"Thank you," Nino said. He stood looking at him. He was repulsive.

"What are you doing to those stamps?" Nino asked.

"Perforating them with the school's initials, C.U. They think it will stop people who work here from stealing stamps."

"It might work," Nino said. "It might work."

"But then again," said Alex, "it makes them more valuable because they're unusual. I think they'll be stolen more this way."

"Unusual things aren't always more valuable," Nino said. "The hardest thing to find nowadays is something perfectly ordinary. Something normal."

Alex looked up at him.

"What's your name?" Nino asked.

"Alex."

"Alex what?" Nino said softly. He could, after all, just walk away.

"Alex Arjine," Alex said, without looking up. He had stamped through the last sheet.

"How do you spell that?" Nino asked, pushing his luck.

"I have to go," said Alex. "I have a class." He reached for a slim book, but Nino picked it up first. *The Language of the Mandarins: A Chinese Grammar.* He checked the title page. Sure enough, the creep had written his name on it.

"You study Chinese affairs?" Nino asked.

"This is just a hobby," Alex said, walking off.

Careless, Nino thought. He's sloppy, leaving that machine with the stamps still in it. Anyone could take them. He paused, lingering over the sheet. And he's foolishly trusting, blabbing about himself like that. He walked farther into the room. He caught sight of Gina typing with her back to him. It's for her own good, he thought. The boy might be bad, or he might not. Chances were that he was, wearing that beard. Nino concluded decisively: a man that will hide his chin will hide anything.

He limped over to her desk and tapped her on the back with the edge of his cane.

"Hello," she said, swiveling around. "What are you doing here?"

"Just going for a walk," he said cheerfully. He was beginning to enjoy himself. It was all so much easier than he had expected. "I thought I might take you to lunch."

Gina looked at him appraisingly. He never did anything for nothing. "Lunch?" she said. "Fine. I thought you were bringing me some more mail," she added, reaching for her bag.

"No letters today," he said. This message, he thought, isn't going to be so easy to read. "What makes you think there were? Expecting anything?"

"I just know how you like to bring me bad news," she said. "When I see you, I think, Is it doomsday today? And then, if there's no such thing as a free lunch, I think, What is this lunch going to cost me? There has to be some bad news."

"Sometimes the news you think is bad turns out to be good news in the long run. It's a question of having the patience to see how it all turns out." That was it, he thought, agreeing with himself; he wanted to see how it all turned out with her. That was the fun of it, but he suspected he wasn't going to be around for the crucial act. "Sometimes the things you think are good to begin with turn out to be rotten," he pontificated genially, sizing her up.

"What did you ever think was good to begin with," she asked, taking her purse from a drawer and getting up.

"Don't fish." He smiled. "Although I will say you were always ready to keep me company when I came home at midnight. Everyone else was asleep, but you, you were ready to talk as soon as you learned a few words."

"Let's eat," she said. There was nothing that bothered her more than Nino in his affectionate phase.

"A real restaurant," he insisted, limping after her. "Not one of those two-carrots-and-ice-water places you go to."

"There's a Greek restaurant down the street," Gina said.

They walked out into the brilliant midday heat. Even the

thick, dusty air couldn't stop the burning impact of the sun. The brick walk seemed to scorch her feet through the thin-soled sandals; the sun seemed to blister her bare arms and throat. It's not the heat, she thought, it's him. She walked slowly, to keep pace with him and to avoid the impulse to run. It wasn't his toughness that scared her, but his need for her obedience, his domineering love, his self-mastery. The neat, immaculate suits, the white shirts and carefully knotted ties he wore in the most intense heat, made her want to scream at his discipline. The dark Sicilian skin, turned gray from illness, the face fixed in sour lines, was lit up now. He has an idea, she thought. It's bringing him around. It has to do with me.

"When you're young," he said expansively, "you never think how wrong everything can go."

"Ignorance is bliss," she said.

"But only knowledge is power," he answered.

"Bliss is better than power," she came back.

"Maybe," he smiled, "but it doesn't last. If you read any of the books I told you to read instead of the trash you waste your time with, you might learn something. Did you ever read that Conrad story, 'Youth'? Now that's the kind of thing you can remember: the boy going out to sea and the ship burning up. . . . 'A high clear flame, an immense and lonely flame, ascended from the ocean, and from its summit,' " Nino chanted, " 'the black smoke poured continuously at the sky. She burned furiously. . . . ' " He was losing the thread. " '. . . A magnificent death had come like grace, like a gift' "— Nino had found the words again—" 'Like a reward . . . like the sight of a glorious triumph.' But then, of course, the ship sinks without a trace. Now that," he said, waving his cane, pleased at remembering so much, "is life."

"It's not exactly all of it," Gina said. "You left out everything that happened before the ship caught fire. And all the other ships that are still around," she added. But the truth was that she admired his cheerful fatalism. He had sounded the depths; his limp proved it. But he too had made a mark; had flattened the depths out a little. Now the consistency with which hopes went under gave him no anguish, no bitterness, but a sense of rightness. That was the good part.

She could see from his easy manner that something was up. He was always compassionate when he was destroying her hopes, as though in bringing her down, he pitied her fall. He drew her into some greater proximity to him—a closeness with fatalism for glue. Already she could feel his dimness gumming up her mood. It was never possible to be with him without getting hurt. He never meant ill, but he always did harm, with an unerring sense of where to strike.

Watching him speak, and linger over the burning of the ship—the ship always burned up under you, the ship that might get you out—she could hardly remember how many times his stories had lured her into some trap, some embarrassment, some moral that added up to her humiliation. There were moments when his face relaxed and she could remember his laughing, playing catch with her, telling her every night the same bedtime story of the bird and the worm.

Was it his stroke that had changed him, or just her growing up? He had been so affectionate when she was little. It seemed as though one morning she woke up and he had changed, become wary, suspicious, remote. Had he always been that way? What difference does it make? She grew up just as the vessels in his brain exploded; she wanted out just as he started going down. His dogged pursuit of her seemed darker, more complex, and more hopeless as each month passed. She knew he was curious about what she was. There had been too many papers disturbed on her desk, too many books placed in the wrong order, too many sudden encounters on the street. Nino never left anything to chance if he could help it.

"Good, isn't it?" Nino demanded, pleased he had remembered the description of the burning ship. "That's English. And he was even a Pole, just an immigrant." Nino nodded, surveying the black kids milling around the steps of an SRO hotel on Broadway. "Superficial differences don't count all that much," he said expansively. He waved his cane over Broadway. "The truth is," he paused, "we're all damned, white souls and black. And who knows the way out of that? Your mother thinks I am too Catholic, that I believe everything the Church says. But the Church has no conscience and no concern." He shook his head.

"You're right," Gina said. Better the Pope than me, she thought wryly, knowing her turn would come to take the heat. "Angelo told me about Maria. That was terrible."

"What did he tell you?" Nino asked suspiciously.

"He told me everything," Gina said.

"What is everything?"

Gina smiled. He had said Nino hauled her body to Mulberry Street and rigged a phony mass, and then decided to lie to the rest of the family about it. He had been sure Nino did it just because it would embarrass him if Maria weren't buried in consecrated ground.

"Just that the priest gave you a hard time before Maria was buried."

"Angelo talks too much. And he doesn't talk sense. I know he told you more than that. Do you think I'm an idiot? I did it because it was the right thing to do. It's not for him to question my motives. Look at him. He's twenty-four and he still thinks like a kid. He goes here, he goes there." Nino gestured. "He looks for a good time; he looks for someone to pop up with a sign that says 'Follow Me!' He's too much of a fool to see the truth is under his nose. I forbid you to talk to him again. When did you see him?"

"At the funeral," Gina answered, amused at how annoyed Nino was.

They passed through the door into the restaurant, Nino leaning heavily on his cane as they went down the four steps. He sighed, motioning toward a table in the corner. "Air conditioning is one of the greatest things in America. A large carafe of white wine," he told the waiter, accepting a menu, but putting it down after a moment. He began to joke with the waiter in Greek. He prided himself on picking up languages. Whenever she glimpsed him with one of his cronies, she realized he was different with them than with anyone at home. He was like that now, questioning the waiter, ordering what he thought was good for her without asking her what she wanted. When the waiter left, Nino turned to her genially, picked up his wine glass, and said, "Salud!"

"Salud!" she returned cautiously.

He seemed amused, looking her over. She had been a beautiful child, he thought, a perfect little face with huge, almond-shaped eyes. Laura always dressed her in starched pinafores—pink and white and yellow. She would flutter through the empty lot next to the house while he watched, yelling at her not to get dirty. But she always got dirty. Whenever she did anything wrong, she would admit it with an air of such utter, innocent trustfulness that it was hard to punish her. Even as a child she was wily, restless, full of will. It had not been easy to change her. But somewhere along the way she had become careful, self-controlled. Even if it takes a lot of belt buckle, you have to teach a girl she can't get what she wants. Otherwise, they're impossible to live with.

But she isn't a kid anymore, he thought mournfully. Her dark hair was long, falling in soft fluffy waves to her shoulders.

She sat opposite him in an immaculate white dress that set off her tanned, smooth skin. Her face had always fascinated him, partly because it was his face, only more delicate, more . . . lovely. She has a really Italian grace, he thought, satisfied. His feeling for her surprised him, rising over his determination to start questioning her right away.

"Why is it that we don't get along better?" he asked softly.

"You're too complicated to get along with," she answered easily. When Nino pleaded for sympathy and understanding, she always wound up taking a beating in the end. Mom always said, 'Never feel sorry for a man; you'll always regret it later on.' But Mom always wound up being taken in. It was better to attack now, she decided. "It's hard to get along with someone who sneaks around, following you to the fruit store. Haven't you got anything better to do?" she said lightly.

Nino took a long sip of wine. "I'm your father. If there is some . . . disturbance in your life, I have a right to know."

"You could ask," Gina suggested.

"I could ask," Nino agreed. "But you wouldn't answer."

"I never refuse to talk to you," Gina said.

"No, you don't. But you know how to keep quiet even while you're talking," Nino said. "So what good are your answers?"

"Silence is golden?" she offered.

"Not yours. I've had enough of that. I know you're hiding something," Nino said finally. "You should know that I am your father, and I . . . I care about you. You should feel the same because you're my daughter. That is the way it's supposed to be. If there is confusion in your life, you should come to me with it so I can set it straight." He patted her hand, his long yellowed nails scraping her skin.

Mercifully, the waiter arrived with platters of food. Nino had ordered squid for both of them. She smiled insincerely, stalling for time. "You do know what I like to eat," she said.

"Something light," he said, watching her. "So you can go on looking like a stick."

"You do know food," she continued, on a safe subject. He did know food. He had eaten himself into diabetes and a stroke. After that she began to live on raw vegetables. She searched his ruined face for some clue to how much he knew. In the cool, sepulchral dimness of the restaurant, she felt she was floating. He leaned toward her again, dark and shriveled like some ancient oracle. There were times when each of them seemed thousands of years old. At Aulis, he would have been the first to volunteer as a stand-in for Agamemnon, dragging her on as Iphigenia. She could see he had put an axe in her future. He was about to drop it on her neck himself, accompanied by a speech full of tenderness and piety and idealism.

"I have nothing to hide," Gina lied. "What makes you think I do?"

"As you pointed out, I'm a sneak and a spy," Nino said, grinning. "We sneaks see everything, unlike you angels, who do nothing."

"What kinds of things do you see?" Gina asked, slicing the longest tentacle.

"This and that," Nino said noncommittally.

Gina put down her knife and fork. "That, I guess, proves you're not a very good sneak, or else that there isn't anything of interest to find." She smiled sweetly.

Nino couldn't help smiling back. With her face lit up like that, her eyes full of questions she wasn't going to ask, her demure white dress, she did look angelic. Even as a child, whenever she had done something wrong, she looked especially angelic. He poured her another glass of wine. She's already becoming a complex Sicilian woman, he thought. She'll be interesting at thirty. But, he reminded himself, the more interesting a woman is, the more misery she brings to everyone around her. An interesting woman is a curse.

"I found some surprising things."

Gina bit into the fleshy upper tentacle.

"Don't you want to know what they are?" Nino asked.

"Not really," Gina said. "I know there's nothing you could tell me that I don't already know. Anyway, don't you think I have a right to some privacy? I work, I'm on my own, I don't see why my feelings or anything else can't be my own. If I felt it concerned you, I would tell you. If it doesn't concern you, I don't think it's any of your business."

"What I decide is my business, is my business," Nino said, amused.

"That's a matter of opinion," Gina answered.

"Nothing is a matter of opinion. I'm your father; so long as you are my daughter, what you do is my business. Only an idiot would think that his life belongs to himself. You think my life belongs to me? You live in a family with other people; what you do affects them. You can't do anything without taking them into account."

"You mean, without taking *you* into account," said Gina.

Nino shrugged.

"What do you want?" Gina asked quietly.

"I want you to tell me the truth."

"The truth about what?"

"The truth about where you are and who you're with every evening."

The trouble with Nino, Gina thought, was that you could never tell if he was just fishing or if he really knew something. If she admitted to something he didn't know, she would give herself away. He would automatically add to whatever she acknowledged, knowing that she wouldn't tell the whole story. If she denied everything, and he knew something, he would assume still worse.

"Sometimes I go to the library; sometimes I see a movie," Gina said. "I've told you that."

"Who do you do these things with?" Nino asked softly.

"Sometimes alone; sometimes with friends I've made at work."

"These friends—are they girls or boys?"

"Mostly girls," Gina said.

"These girls," Nino asked, leaning forward, "how many of them have beards?"

So he knows. He knows a lot. "All of them," Gina said conspiratorially, "every one."

Nino looked grayer than ever.

"Cheer up," Gina said. "I've answered all your questions, haven't I?"

"I haven't begun to ask questions," Nino answered sourly. "Look how you treat this, as though it were a joke. It's not a joke." He tightened his fist around his cane.

"You aren't going to use that on me in public, are you?" Gina said.

"I don't want to use it at all. I'm giving you a chance to be honest."

"Now that I've taken it, let me tell you again that my feelings are my own. Not yours." She sliced the air with her hand, to cut him off from her.

He looked at her, little Gina, talking like a tough and hardened stranger. She had finished all the squid, eating it like someone determined to survive an ordeal. She had his firmness; he realized she would never tell him anything, any more than he would have admitted anything in her place. Her silence, it came to him, was proof of his effect upon her. She was his daughter; she was too much like him. It made it hard for him to go further, to go as far as he knew he would have to.

She could see how troubled he was. It was beginning to

get to her. He had taken the trouble to be civilized, to speak to her directly. It wasn't the worst he could have done, and yet it was getting him nowhere. She could sympathize with how he felt, but that was it. It was clear that he wanted to be loved; he didn't want to ruin it completely by giving in to his rage. She could see his anger flickering on and off—it was hard for him to sustain it, even though she was giving him nothing. It came upon her that his sense of failure must be terrible.

"Dad," she said, leaning forward, "give it up. It's not what you think, and it's not worth it for you. Things will always be the same between us, whatever else I do. You have to let it go, or you'll make it impossible for both of us."

"How can things be the same when you're so entirely different? How can I stand by and watch you ruin everything through stupidity?"

"I'm not stupid."

"People who think they're smart enough to manage anything usually turn out to be wrong."

"If the worst you could imagine were true, what would be such a big deal? What difference would it make to anyone but you?"

"You're the one who will pay the price, Gina. It will make a difference to you. You may think it won't now, but you'll find out differently. What will you do with yourself? Did you think of that? I let you go to college"—he hesitated, seeing her wince at "let you"—"but do you think you'll ever finish? Girls who play with fire burn up their diplomas."

"So you've decided that school is the lesser of two evils?" she asked.

Nino nodded.

"Don't worry, Dad," Gina said, taking his hand. "I'm too stubborn to flunk out." She smiled. The truth was, she suspected he wanted her to succeed in college as much, maybe even more, than she did. He just wouldn't admit it. She stood up.

"Sit down," he ordered. He was losing patience. She complied. "What is it you are doing, what is it you want? Do you want to marry this man?"

"What man?"

"The one you don't see every night."

"I don't want to marry him. I just want peace between you and me," she said with finality.

She checked her watch and stood up. "Enjoy your lunch," she said. "I have to get back, but there's no need for you to rush. And thanks." She took his hand for a moment, then turned and walked out into the yellow heat.

Nino, for the first time, felt his assurance fading. How she had looked him straight in the eye and patted his hand, as though he were ninety. As though he were a fool! His tenderness, rising even with his irritability, had crippled him. She had spoiled for him the desire to let her down with magnanimity. It flashed through his mind that he could go back to confront her and the boy at the office. That would be really bad for her, to do it in front of everyone. Just the sight of him with Gina would be enough to slow this Alex down, if not stop him. Somehow, when Gina had been with him, putting her in place didn't seem so important. The minute she had gone, his responsibility came thudding on his brain. He had come all the way here and done nothing. Now he would have to take one more step to salvage the day. He sat back, enjoying the cool whiteness of the restaurant walls, heavily stuccoed and decorated at various points with dark copper bells. The waiter sat at a back table, drinking black coffee and fingering amber worry beads between sips. A black silk tassel hung from the beads, shimmering as he turned them. You could understand a man like that. Nino

waited until the man had finished circling the string before
signaling him for coffee and a check. Gina's business could
wait until tomorrow, he thought, sipping the thick, bitter
coffee. I've done enough for today.

The pins-and-needles sensation in his feet was constant
now, worsening as he moved on toward 125th Street and the
bus across the Triboro to Queens. By the time he had walked
up Amsterdam to the Casa Italiana he was already exhausted.
Less than five blocks, he thought bitterly, pausing by the
door. It was almost eighteen years since he'd been president
of the Dante Circle, and Columbia had rented them space
there to hold socials and lectures. Memories hurled themselves
at him, but the ones that hit were of dances, waltzes where
he whirled around with girls in low-backed dresses, politely
keeping his distance even while he held them, wearing gloves
or holding a handkerchief between his hand and the smooth
bare backs. Some of those girls. . . . His fingers played over
the beautifully carved wooden door. He could picture the
foyer inside: carved mahogany molding, deep-rust quarry
tile, high cream-colored ceilings.

He limped forward, his leg too numb already to think of
making another stop. What's over is over, he thought. When
he stopped feeling the sensation of jabbing pins, he would
feel nothing. Later, at home, he hoisted his bad leg—it was
getting hard to tell which one it was—onto the sofa. Better
bad circulation than none, he thought. He took off his shoes
and socks and reached for the iodine he kept in his pocket.
Someone had told him it would ward off infection. He began
painting his gray toes with it. When he finished, he switched
on the television set, wincing from the sting, but pleased that
he still felt something. Thank God he had gotten Nunzio to
check out the jerk at the Motor Vehicles Bureau for him. He
couldn't face a trip down there in the morning. But as it was,
coming and going had cost him the entire afternoon. He had

missed most of the ball game. The Yankees were winning, but not by much. He nodded grimly. It still wasn't over. The game's not over 'til it's over! The Red Sox were only down one in the seventh inning. He settled back to watch. When Laura came in she found him cheering, goading, "Get 'em! Get 'em!"

Another game, the same noise, Laura thought. Football, baseball, they followed one another season after season, keeping the noise level constant. The nasal-voiced announcers screaming into mikes, the raucous crowds, the tense cheers into the television set. . . . She put the heavy bags of groceries on the kitchen table. It would be wonderful to come home to quiet. Or maybe conversation. But you could never really tell him anything over the noise. He kept on watching the screen while you talked, and you never knew what he meant by his irritable answers. Sports anger—it was one of the terrible things a woman discovers in marriage.

"What's new?" Laura asked anyway, coming into the living room. She waited, but no answer came. "You want something?"

"No, no," Nino said, clenching his teeth.

"I have beautiful grapefruit," Laura coaxed. "Smell," she insisted, holding one out to him.

"No, no. Can't you see, I'm watching the game."

"You watched the game yesterday," Laura pointed out.

"This is a different game."

"Would you rather have yellow grapefruit or pink grapefruit?"

"I don't want any grapefruit!"

"You never have an opinion about anything important," Laura said. "That's what's wrong with you." She was back in a minute, peeling a tangerine and putting the peels in a bowl of water. "Don't you love the smell of tangerines?" she asked. "It fills the room."

"That's it!" Nino screamed. "Strike him out! That does it!"

Laura looked at the set. It seemed to be over, but he would still want to watch the interviews in the locker rooms. Then a bunch of men would sit around talking about the game. It never ended. Usually she was more resigned, but today there were too many things on her mind. She went to work in the kitchen, pulling the ends off smooth green beans, breaking the beans in half and plopping them into a bowl. Wonderful vegetables, she thought, really firm.

She was supposed to write down a recipe for Mrs. Gourkas, she remembered. Spinach pie. First you go to Gino for two pounds of fresh spinach, take it home, and wash it. No: first you go to Leo's for a loaf of Italian bread and let it get stale. No, no, you buy the bread the day before so the spinach doesn't get soft. Then by the time you buy the spinach, the bread feels stale. Then you clean the spinach and chop it. Separate four eggs and beat up the whites; grate the bread into crumbs and add some melted butter and heavy cream beaten with the yolks. Then you put in some grated parmesan and that's it. She ought to be able to do that, Laura thought.

And then she had promised Luisa she would get Nino's advice about Millie. Although what good his advice would do was beyond her. Sometimes, Laura conceded, his judgment wasn't bad. She listened to the post-game roundup from the kitchen. The Yankees seemed to have won. Thank God. You can't talk to him when they lose. She waited until the last thing had been said about the game, and went into the living room just as he was reaching for the radio. How many post-game roundups can he want, she thought irritably. She waited, nevertheless, as he tried station after station, arranging the rubber-backed throw so that it covered the sofa. Striped gold and green, it had absorbed countless dots of iodine and sustained several cigarette burns, while, she thought gratefully, the sofa remained OK.

"Today," Laura began when she saw there was nothing on the radio about the game, "Luisa from the old neighborhood called me. She has such trouble because of Millie, her daughter. You remember? The plain one?"

"I don't remember either of them," Nino admitted.

"You remember," Laura insisted. "Luisa, the widow, who lived over the bakery. She had a boy, Frankie, and a girl, Millie."

Nino shrugged, glancing at the light reflecting from the white ceramic lamp on the end table. The lamp was always on, because the ground-floor apartment was so dark. Even in summer, Nino defended it: it's dark, which is good, because that keeps it cool.

"Let me begin at the beginning," Laura said, sitting back in the wooden rocker that faced the sofa.

"I don't see why you should begin," Nino said reasonably, "because I don't remember who you're talking about."

"They remember you," Laura said. "Luisa wanted your opinion of what happened to Millie. She thinks," Laura continued too foolishly innocent to take the doubt from her voice, "that you know a lot about life. If I don't begin, then I'll never finish."

Nino settled back, putting his feet on the sofa so that they would be sure to miss the hideous throw. "If she wants my opinion, I'll give her my opinion," he said.

"Now Millie," Laura began, "lived with her mother on Mulberry Street, over Grito's bakery. Her father had worked for the post office, but while Millie was in the last year of high school, he died. Her mother had very little money, since all she had was the annuity she received from the post office. When Millie graduated high school, she had trouble finding a job because she was plain, shy, and she had no skills. So Luisa borrowed money from her Uncle Gabriel to send her to the Katharine Gibbs secretarial school. Millie didn't want to go, but Luisa forced her. But Millie worked hard and when she graduated the school found her a job. Her mother said, 'Millie, when you get paid, give me your salary and I will save some of it for you. Someday, when you get married, you can spend it on your apartment. I will give you an allowance each week.'

"Just the mention of this made Millie mad. 'You know I will never get married,' Millie would scream. 'I never even had a boyfriend.' Now her brother, Frank, was going to the Delehanty Institute to be stretched, so he could pass the height test to be a policeman. Whenever there was a dance or a meeting, Luisa would tell Frank, 'Take you sister! Introduce her to your friends.' But Frank always refused. 'It's not my responsibility,' he'd say. 'It's not my fault she's ugly.'

"But a girl Millie met at work invited her to her wedding. The bride knew, through her mother, a widower who was looking for a good girl to marry because he needed someone to care for his three children. The bride introduced them at the wedding, and to make a long story short, the man saw that Millie was simple and plain, and thought she would be perfect."

"So what was the problem?" Nino asked.

"That's what I'm getting to," Laura went on uneasily. "When Millie told Luisa about him, she told her to forget him. She knew Millie was too lonely and nervous to take care of someone else's kids, and besides, why should her daughter, just because she was plain, be a housekeeper for someone else's family. But Millie was lonely and since no one else had ever bothered with her, she began to see the man secretly. To make a long story short, she took off hours from her job, and she sneaked around until she was fired. Luisa suspected something was wrong. So one day she followed her—"

"You mean," Nino interrupted, "Frankie didn't do this for her?"

"No," Laura said. "You know how the boys are these days. He didn't want to get involved."

Nino shook his head. Women were no good at these things, but what could they do when the men didn't do the right thing? Frankie was old enough to look out for his sister, if there was no father.

"So Luisa," Laura continued, "followed her and caught her meeting the man on the street. Now Millie was high-strung. She had had . . . little breakdowns . . . before, but when Luisa caught her, she just blew up. The man said he would stand by her and told her to move in with him and his mother. He persuaded Millie that since his mother was there, it would be all right. He told her that if things worked out and she liked the children, they would get married. But"—Laura leaned forward—"I don't think he really meant it. He really just wanted to see if Millie could run the family."

Nino nodded.

"Things went well until one day when the man's mother fell off a ladder while she was hanging the kitchen curtains. She was taken to Saint Vincent's where they said she had a broken hip. Millie was left alone to take care of the children. They made her so nervous, they set off her condition. One day the man came home and found her screaming and throwing things. The children were hiding under the kitchen table and behind the living-room chairs. He couldn't believe that even the policemen the neighbors called had trouble controlling her."

"What happened to her?" Nino asked.

"The man was through with her. He could see she was no good with children. So he had the cops do what they wanted, which was to take her to Bellevue. Then he went to see Luisa and told her Millie was in the hospital and it was up to her

to sign the papers. She gave him a piece of her mind. 'I knew
you would ruin her,' she told him.

" 'I didn't ruin her,' the man said. 'I never even touched
her.' " Laura paused, disturbed.

"That's a terrible story," Nino said. He was wondering why
she had told it to him, and whether she knew about Gina.

"Luisa is very troubled about things she can't figure out.
She wanted to ask a man, but a priest wouldn't know. So she
asked me to ask you because she thought . . . in your line of
work . . . you might have had the experience."

"Everything in the story is disturbing," Nino agreed, flat-
tered. "What is it particularly that bothers her?"

"It's the man, the widower. Do you think he is telling the
truth when he says he never touched Millie?"

Nino looked at Laura. "You mean, after all that, that is
what bothers her?"

"Yes," Laura said. "Even I wonder. Do you think he touched
her?"

Nino thought for a minute. "No," he said. "I don't."

The truth was, it *was* a big issue. It was one thing to take
advantage of somebody's trust to make them take care of a
house and children, but another to use a girl for everything,
without even marrying her. Nino knew what this kind of man
was like—he probably didn't touch her because he was
touching someone else on the side, someone who was pretty,
while the plain one at home did all the work. It bothered
him that women were so dumb that they let men like this
take advantage of them. There was no justice in it. It was
true the women were the ones who took the beating. But it
was, after all, their fault for not demanding marriage first,
so at least they would have respectability. But some of them
never had the stamina to hold out—not without a father
making sure they did. After all, Millie got what she deserved.
Still, it was sad. Millie had no father, and a brother who was

good for nothing. Her mother tried, but what good are women in situations like that? Millie was simple and wrong, but she was, it seemed, not really perverse. Gina was another matter. She seemed so cold, so brittle, so much in control— not at all the type to get involved in such a lousy business. But how could anything be certain? Who is to say that she wouldn't do something crazy even if she knew, clearly, that it was crazy? He looked at Laura appraisingly. There was something more to this. Why had she told him this story?

"Why did you really tell me this story?" he asked Laura gently.

"Luisa wanted me to," Laura said, but she seemed agitated. She wasn't that close to Luisa.

"Isn't there another reason?" he coaxed, taking her hand. "Yes?" he persisted softly. You can catch more flies with honey than vinegar. He could see her wavering. She would never learn to keep her mouth shut.

"There was another reason," Laura began hesitantly.

Nino waited, rubbing his foot against the back of the sofa.

"It's Gina. She's . . . different lately."

"Different?" Nino prodded. "In what way?"

"She's more . . . mature. It's true she's working, but that's not it. She's away all the time. When she comes home at night, she's always happy. When she goes out, she dresses so carefully. Even if I leave before her, I can see from how everything is left that she tries on everything before she decides what to wear. And . . . she doesn't look like a young girl anymore."

Nino darkened. That he hadn't picked up. This was the nail in the coffin. By the time anything hit Laura, it must be more obvious than the Empire State Building. What had made him so easy on Gina!

"Do you think she's involved with someone?" Nino brought out.

"I found this," Laura said, taking a photograph from her handbag. It was a color picture of Gina and that Alex at some kind of dinner party. They were sitting at a round table in a restaurant, with a few other people. The boy's arm rested on the back of her chair. They were not looking into the camera. Nino shook his head. They were smiling at each other. Nino studied the picture carefully, as though it were a code, complex but not indecipherable. In a peculiar way the boy was attractive. He was elegant. Amazing what a suit and tie will do for anyone! His hair and beard were so perfectly clipped there wasn't a hair out of place. He was fair; his intensely white skin made the yellow of his hair and beard seem even brighter. Gina's profile was striking—her heavy black lashes, straight nose, and long dark hair were set off by a white silk blouse. Always in white, the little bitch! Her skin was rosy and olive. They made an interesting pair: his pallor, her darkness. They were, he concluded, a couple. The demure correctness of their clothes couldn't mislead him. Look how casually the boy's arm rests on the back of her chair, his hand brushing her shoulder. Look how easily she remains within his reach, looking up at him, amused. There was an intimacy there, a heat that had been satisfied. What a fool he had been to give her the benefit of the doubt.

"How long have you had this?" Nino asked.

"Four or five weeks."

"Do you know anything about this boy?"

"Not really."

"What do you know?" Nino prodded, still keeping his voice low.

"Just that she met him at work. That's a luncheon they had for someone who left." She pointed to the picture.

"Did you question her about him?" Nino asked softly.

"I thought she had a right to her privacy. The boy didn't seem to mean very much to her," Laura said lamely.

"Did you expect her to provide you with films of the two of them alone together?" Nino demanded.

"Don't jump to conclusions," Laura whispered.

"You must suspect something yourself. Is that why you told me that story about Millie and Luisa?"

"You can't compare Gina to Millie," Laura said irritably. The trouble was, you could. It always seemed to come down to what a girl went through and what a man got away with. From the time you were born it was drummed into you. If the radio was on the Italian stations, you heard about it. If you wanted music, it was there. Her father had taken her to see *Rigoletto*, and she could remember every scene as though she had seen it that morning. The last act could give you nightmares. There was Gilda, kept too sheltered, and then taken advantage of by the worthless duke. There she was, dying for that skirt-chasing rapist while *he* sang about the fickleness of women. Every time she thought of it, it made her angry. It's true nothing like that had ever happened to her; still, it touched something at the heart of things. There were people who went through life skimming the cream, and others who paid the price. The first were most of them men, the second were mostly women. The women in the opera had to die before the men would even realize their mistake. Poor Violetta, Gilda, Concetta's pregnant young daughter. And all for what?

The women went under because they were lonely and looking for something to give their lives some purpose, a cause that always seemed to take the shape of some Nino. Now she could see it. Not for nothing had she lived this long! Nino had always been so sure of everything, so solid. That was what you expected in a man. You married him and then—she shook her head—you had to live with him and you found out what it really meant. Nino made her feel lonely all the time. When you have to get along with a dictator, something inside you dies; there is never a free, easy, peaceful moment. What will he say? What will he do? If you go to the fruit store, you worry about getting back when he expects you and it spoils the conversation with women you meet. If you stay home, he crowds all your time, deciding what you should do, when you should do it, always interrupting with his needs. There was no closeness because he made himself such an object of fear it was impossible to be anything but angry or silent. That was just the way it was. But she hadn't counted on anything going wrong with Gina. This boy was a mistake. He would shame them all. It was making her sick. She had done all she knew how for her. Now, in return for that, she was going to wind up wringing her hands, one of those mothers like Luisa who was always asking for sympathy.

Nino, she could see, was brooding. He sat, too enraged and depressed for words. Whatever was happening, he would make worse. Some things were certain: the sofa he could never keep covered; the ball games that never ended; the men talking after the game, of scores, injuries, comebacks.

"You," Laura said suddenly, "you caused this. If you hadn't hounded and humiliated her all her life, she wouldn't be so rebellious. She knows what's good for her."

Nino barely heard her.

"You forced this on all of us, the way you behave. Who do you think you are! Bringing that letter to school, making fun of everything she wants to do. No wonder she kept everything to herself. Why should she give you any more ammunition than you've already got?"

Nino stared, rage flowing from his filmy eyes.

"You remember how my father tied my younger sister to the bedpost so she couldn't go out when he was away for the evening? That's what you did to her."

"I never tied anyone up. I am not like that," Nino said hoarsely. "That is not civilized."

"No wonder she wants to be free," Laura said in a strange, flat voice. "That's what you did to me, too." She could see Nino had tears in his eyes. What did it matter now? "You made both of us feel tied up. I've felt that way for thirty years."

"What you feel has nothing to do with me," Nino said, speaking slowly, as if he could barely form the words. "You would have felt that way no matter who you married. You wouldn't know what to do with yourself without being told." He waved his arm, taking in the living room: the beige walls, the round Queen Anne mirror over the convertible sofa, the wedding picture of Laura in an elaborate lace and satin gown, holding a huge bouquet of calla lilies, Maria's phonograph with three legs and a stack of books for the fourth. "I've given you a life," Nino declared. "Without me, what would you have done? Who would have organized you, given you a purpose?"

Laura began to cry.

Nino pressed on. "You think you missed something. You didn't. You, you, don't you see, you did this to Gina because you were never at peace with yourself. You egged her on, encouraging her to do this, do that. You gave her your dissatisfaction with everything. You taught her to disrespect me."

"She didn't need me to teach her that!" Laura snapped. "And I didn't need you to tell me when to get up and when to go to sleep, when to eat dinner and when to go shopping. I could have figured those things out for myself!"

"You infected her with a disease. Like smallpox," Nino went on, ignoring her. "First you get one sore, then another, then you're covered with them. This is the one we found out about," Nino hissed, pounding the boy's picture. "There may be others. With girls, rebellion always means the same thing." He fell back, weary. "Once it happens, there's no going back to the way things were before. Like the stroke, it comes, takes a little of your sight, leaves you a little crippled, and goes. But there you are. Stuck for the rest of your life."

"She's not sick, and nobody's stuck for the rest of their life because of one mistake," Laura protested. "Not if she's not pregnant, she's not stuck."

"No," Nino said. "The fact that she did this means we've lost her. We failed; it's as simple as that." His voice trailed off. How she must have hated him to do this! How she must have been mocking him all the while, making a fool of him in bed with that . . . thing! "She betrayed me!" Nino brooded.

"How could she betray you? You're her father, not her husband! She must have been lonely, that's all."

"She betrayed me," Nino repeated, "and you, you helped her." He leaned forward menacingly. "But now you're going to help me. Because you need me to get her out of this and you know it." Nino grabbed her hands. "If you didn't know that, you wouldn't have shown me that picture, would you?"

Three

She could see him in the distance, trying to hide behind a newspaper as he sat on the bench in front of the ruins of P.S. 5. For days she had caught glimpses of him reflected in store windows. Turning suddenly she had caught sight of him limping into a doorway or stepping back deeper into a subway car. He was unmistakably there now, waiting to see where she would go. He was still at it. Once or twice you could meet Nino by chance. But this was something else. I haven't fooled him at all, she realized. How long had he been doing this, watching her drop off a weekly supply of unread books before, dressed demurely as a Catholic schoolgirl, she went to meet Alex and strip?

Gina stepped back into the library, unable to decide what to do. Should she meet Alex anyway? Should she try to lose Nino on the train? Should she call his shot and just confront him? Should she spend the evening in the library and make Nino wait for nothing? What was the right thing to do?

If he wants to follow me, I'll give him a chase he won't

forget, Gina thought grimly. It came to her, the determination to make him run, run, run in the sunlight that was still hotter than kisses. It came like a fire itself, freeing and fueling her rage. Who was he not to believe what she said? He wouldn't stand for the truth; he wouldn't stand for her lying. So let him not stand at all, let him exhaust himself until he couldn't tell the difference between truths and lies. A war was a war. Once he realized he wasn't going to win, he would give up.

Gina moved out onto the library steps, walking slowly so that he would be sure to see her. What if he didn't get up? What if he were only reading the paper? Geared for war, the possibility of a missed fight wasn't what she wanted. But she could tell now for sure, seeing him gathering himself together, that he was following. She moved toward the station, deliberately crossing the street so that he could climb the long staircase of the El without fear that she would see him. The shaded stairway seemed cool; out on the subway platform the sun shone down on the hot, splintering wood. She loved this platform. From the end, looking over the dome of Saint Demetrios's Church, she could see the New York skyline, suspended in the shimmering heat.

On the street below were the private houses, the six-story apartments, the little yards overpacked with rosebushes and fig trees—the vestigial village beyond which the city stood like a mirage. Were you thirsty? The city was water. Were you low? It was all height and promise. Were you lonely? There was Alex. She could hardly keep her mind on Nino. That was the trouble with Nino. When he was around, he focused everything. When he was gone, it seemed as though he didn't exist at all. I'm not, she realized, purposeful enough for a good vendetta. I don't want revenge, I want out. But there he was, committed to pursuit to the last drop of blood. She looked away, into the rosebushes pinned and pruned on their trellises.

It was the month they call in Sicily the time of the lion sun. There the heat ruled without rivals. Here in Astoria the rose-packed gardens hurled sweetness into the dust-laden air, the smells of cooking bubbled from open kitchen windows into streets pungent with car exhausts, the El rained soot on the street below; all seemed fused into a seething life that was fair match for the ravenous sun. The BMT went crashing around the curve from Hoyt Avenue, its wheels grinding to an ear-splitting stop on the hot rails. Gina got on the train. Peering through the filmy car window she saw Nino limping into the next car. She settled nervously into a seat facing the Manhattan skyline, still visible through the streaked windows as the train screeched on.

There it was. At work, every day, in the city, typing past-due bills, or letters politely requesting payment, the beauty of it receded before the familiar routine of drudge-work. But even the bills she typed sometimes seemed launched into that other world where people lived gracefully, lightly, never paying their dues. Not my lot, she thought wistfully. With Nino your bills were always due. You could meet them on the infinite installment plan. Pay-as-you-go-to-the-grave in regular portions of work, marriage, christenings, funerals. Spellbound you paid and paid. What made it all work for so long? What was the magic? The sense of fear? Just fear of Nino's rages, the wreckage he made with his words and his cane? It was part of it. You couldn't shortchange his menacing voice and punishing ways. But it wasn't that alone that made it seem impossible to default on Nino. He had an air of being right. Nino! she wanted to scream. You can't collect from me! But his air of certainty made her feel doubtful, confused. How could you set your confusion against all his conviction? And so she felt only a sense of faint dread, a sudden exhaustion that paralyzed the will to cross him. Her weariness came before the fight, making it all seem hopeless before it had begun.

The train plunged into the tunnel that brought not a darkness but only a harsher light. The fluorescent rods, exposed through the broken shields, showed the ragged papers and soot swirling slowly as the train lumbered under the river. The thought of the river overhead, the oily surface stained by chaotically moving tides, pressing its weight year after year against the concrete and steel, never failed to bring the question to mind: When would it give? When would it break, when would the barricade yield passage beneath the surface, finally giving way to the tides? It was a kid's thought. It should have passed long ago. But it didn't. In Sicily, near Amerina, there was a lake, Pergusa, where Hades was supposed to have risen to go foraging for a woman. When he kidnapped Persephone, he took her back through the milky water to the underground place, the hell that was his to rule. Her trip through the water—suspended, airless in alien hands—must have been terrifying. It was just a story, a story without a place in a subway car inscribed with graffiti. Yet it stayed in her mind like the image of Nino in the next car.

The train was really speeding now, rocking into the bright blue bulbs that lit the tunnel's sides. She could see herself moving toward the door that led to his car, forcing it open, feeling the hot wind between the cars, standing before him, screaming hello over the noise. Maybe that would be the best. The train lurched violently to one side, hurling her against the seat. It hadn't been much of an idea, anyway. Whatever she said, he would refuse to acknowledge; he wouldn't seem even slightly surprised. That would end the ride, but he'd take it as her capitulation, her recognition that he had found her out.

By now, Nino had read the sports news so many times he

remembered it even better than usual, and he usually remembered it all. After the train had passed Bloomingdale's, his curiosity and suspicion rose. He hadn't thought she was going shopping, but still, he nodded, fanning himself with the *News*, you never know. She was, he could see, leaning forward and stretching by the window, arching back in her seat, staring at the lights in the tunnel. When Union Square came and went, he saw her rise.

Eighth Street, he thought. She could catch him on that stop easily, if she hesitated after getting out. He would have to move quickly to avoid getting caught in the door. The absence of a crowd, the midday silence of the station, all gave him pause. He was so easy to spot, a crippled old man. But she moved very quickly, without looking back when she left the station. Heading west, she stopped at the corner, waiting for the light to change. She walked slowly, glancing in store windows. She stopped near University Place, studying the display carefully. He ducked into the doorway of a butcher shop, watching her through a rack of prime rib roasts until she finished windowshopping and went on, turning down University Place. Hobbling quickly, he glanced into the window to see what had made her stop so long. Red lace bras with feathers sprouting from the top, transparent bikini underpants with little red lips embroidered on them, black see-through camisoles, some with cutouts where the nipples would be—Nino clenched his teeth, dug his cane into the sidewalk, and marched on.

She was heading into Washington Square Park. In the heat, only the elegant mansions on the north side seemed to remain intact. Everything else seethed, bubbled. Once, Nino thought, peering at her from behind a tree, this was a potter's field, just a burying ground for the poor. Now, he thought disgustedly, looking at the addicts, winos, and stoned drifters lying on the grass, it looks as though the bodies have surfaced

again. There she was in the middle of it all, buying a soda
from a vendor, drinking on a bench in the blistering sun.
You could barely see south to Judson Church, the fog of
marijuana was so dense. The noise of conga drums, rude
and numbing, thudded through the heat. She sipped her
diet soda, taking it all in. He edged behind her, moving
behind a tree so that even if she turned she couldn't spot
him.

Glancing up, Nino met Garibaldi's eye. There the statue
was, newly whitewashed in its frozen stride. Garibaldi stood
balanced on his right foot, his left leg about to move forward;
his right hand was poised on the sword strapped to his left
side. Was he taking it out of the sheath, or putting it in?
Politics aside, that was the kind of man you could see would
use his sword to defend the right things. But the question
came back. Was he drawing his sword against some tyrant,
or was he putting it away because he had already won? The
face, whitewashed of its lines, smoothed by rains and snows,
couldn't tell you much anymore. But the stance was proud,
a gentleman's stance without being showy. There he was,
after all these years, a warrior with a paunch, not too proud
when he had to leave Italy to help out Meucci, the inventor,
in his candle factory in Staten Island. And then even after
going back to Italy to lead victorious armies, to keep writing
to Meucci as "Dear Boss"!

Nino shook his head. There was a man for you. And people
say Italians are lousy fighters, never able to go the distance.

Gina's hands held the can of soda like a chalice. She had
the mentality of a three-year-old, Nino thought, shaking his
head. He had taken her here through the park so many times
on the way to Aunt Tonetta's. They had even sat on the
bench where she sat now. In those days he didn't have to
hide behind her! He had bought the ice cream pop, the soda,
the lemon ice she had held so solemnly. He had sat with her,

telling her stories, or rushing her along so they wouldn't be late. The new playground on the south side, with its fancy swings and fake hills, hadn't been there.

Rising, turning, Gina glimpsed Nino's face, darkened with sentiment, still turned toward the statue. Garibaldi again, she thought disgustedly. The whitewashed statue was already flecked and pitted with soot, chips had fallen from the pedestal where skateboards had crashed into it. Yet the sight of him had always made Nino gab. What hypocrisy, a petty tyrant like him talking about a liberator. She stuffed the straw into the soda can with her right fist. Striding toward a garbage basket, she hurled the soda into it through a mass of bees hunting for sugar. She had to walk slowly, she realized, or he would lose her, fall too far behind in the winding streets that he used to take her through on the way to visit relatives whose hearts and mouths were always open. By now, each had had his appointed funeral and gone on.

Nino moved after her as she walked south, ambling across West Third, he only dimly realizing they were on their way past Aunt Tonetta's on Thompson Street. How he remembered the wine she used to make, thick as chocolate and half as sweet, bubbling in soda glasses a third full of Seven-Up. Past the lemon ice stand, past the old playground, she crossed Houston, pausing by Saint Anthony's Church. She was moving south. Where was she going? But the question faded as memories hit, as his shirt dampened and ran with sweat in the heat, his neatly knotted tie under the starched collar wet as a marathon runner's sweatband. No more village now. No hotpants, no serapes. The little boys of six and seven in shorts, squatting to draw circles for games of war on the sidewalk, older boys wrapping tape on a broomstick, kids playing boxball, seemed like new versions of old snapshots of himself. His glasses steamed. His rage faded; he kept on, propelled as much by his past as by her. So many mirrors in so many strange faces. Now she was moving east, backtracking, weaving between Spring Street and Houston.

Suddenly she was gone. On the right an empty lot studded with refuse, wild grass, old bottles. On the left an almost unbroken row of tenements. He knew she hadn't reached the corner. He covered the block again. There it was, a narrow alley. Jersey Street? Maybe through here. As he went in, it widened to almost six feet, cutting through the center of the block, virtually paved with broken glass. Green beer-bottle glass, brown glass from other beers, and clear long shards lay shining on the cobblestones in patches where the sun knifed through the alley, all gleaming, even in the shadows. He dragged his left foot gingerly, afraid of falling into the shimmering, cutting edges. Halfway through he realized where he was. He was moving toward the old cathedral on Prince and Mott. He could see ahead of him the chin-high wall of rust-colored brick, the sagging wooden door painted shut to the rectory's back entrance. In the old country the priests could confuse you. There was an old saying: The hand raised in benediction was also the hand that took bread from your mouth. Here in the old days the Irish priests just drenched you with contempt. He grasped the cool, shaded brick wall of the alley. The alley, he remembered, had always been here. Once it had a street sign— Jersey Street? Maybe not. Anyway, it was long gone. He was losing his balance, leaning against the wall as his bad leg, numbed, came to rest. Without going farther, he could picture what was outside. The sagging wooden door would blend into the old brick wall continuing the length of Prince Street, turning the corner at Mott and circling the block, enclosing the old garden cemetery of Saint Patrick's. He forced himself onward, spotting Gina as she slowly reached the corner, letting her hand drift along the hot brick wall. Her dark hair, brushed back by the hot breeze, her white skirt flaring over curving hips, her bare brown legs, sandaled feet—she looked achingly familiar, one of the girls he would have watched forty years ago, leaning against the hot brick wall with his friends. Teasing, cajoling, from the safety of the gang they would call, entice, never getting a response.

He was never very good at it. He was much too shy for even the most promiscuous to pay any attention to him. Yet, in the end, it had paid off. Meeting Mariana, the baker's daughter, on the subway, she had trusted him. For days and evenings after that, they met out of the neighborhood, touched in alleys they didn't know. He could almost feel her soft cotton blouse, smell her rosewatered body, feel the beads of wetness on her arms in the summer heat, in the sun that was hotter than caresses. He grasped the rough brick wall. Mariana that night, that last night when they had gone to Coney Island and stayed, walking under the boardwalk at nightfall. He swallowed painfully. How silky her breasts, her belly had been against the cooling, grainy sand.

This was ridiculous. He forced himself to move against the dizziness, the blinding dizziness of the yellow sun, the rods of light forcing their way between the tenements across the street into his eyes. They were tearing now. Suddenly the air seemed to be thickening. To move was to move against a vapor-wall filled with ghosts, ghost smells, ghost memories rising from the cemetery like the scent of dreams and nightmares. The DelMonte funeral home, still there—a good business, death!—the grocer with his cheeses and salamis—the store that had sold espresso pots and china had given way to dry goods. But nowhere was Gina to be seen.

Nino circled the block, moving toward the main entrance of Saint Patrick's. How many years since he had been inside! His eyes raked the cemetery. She wasn't there, browsing among the tombstones or the ill-kept grass. How nice it had once been, with sprinklers going all the time and Father

Montale planting herbs to border the path. He had a regular collection: thyme, sweet basil, dill; and even, hidden away from view, so nobody would get the wrong idea, a grape arbor concealed behind a ramshackle fence at the corner.

Nino fell back quickly against the wall as he opened the door. So there she was. She was reading the names of people who had donated stained-glass windows to the church. The yellow light, pouring through the brilliant blue and red glass, lit the interior in an odd, garish way. How dusty it seemed inside. The cream-colored walls and painted spindle fences around the altar somehow looked out of place. There was not enough marble in this country to make a proper show when they built this, Nino thought. He edged back out the door, hiding behind it, waiting for her to leave.

In the chapel in back of the church he had married Laura. He swallowed; his throat felt painfully parched. How different his life might have been if he had married Mariana. He had been young and a great dancer. And she was luscious, sweet, voluptuous. It was the summer. The New York summer sweated sex even out of a dead man. He sighed, looking up when the church door slammed. Gina was striding down the walk leading to Mott Street. He rose, limping after her. In the old days he could have outsprinted her for miles, miles, miles. If he had married Mariana, she wouldn't be here at all, he mused. Mariana. It was better not to wonder what had happened to her. How could he have married her, after all? She had let him have his way with her without being married. If she was willing to do that, she could have done it with someone else while married to him. Once you cross a line, you keep crossing. That was human nature.

Nino limped forward. The air was almost unbreathable. All the exhausts of the city, the basements exhaling roach poisons, the fumes of cars, the light pollen of surviving grasses, the rolling dust and soot flurries, were crashing in his lungs. And look at her, that bitch. His suit jacket too was drenched now, sopping and stuck to his body on the shadeless street. And she, running on, gliding over the sidewalks in bare legs and sandals, her white dress still white.

He began to cough, a slow wracking cough, spewing out the city vapors, the memories that stuck like tar in his throat. She moved down Mott past the pork butcher's store on Spring Street, where hams and sausages hung from rope over the white porcelain display; on she went past Kenmare Street, past the liquor shop on Broome with a window full of Mondavi reds, *Zinfandel* in blackish letters on a paper banner. There, she was slowing, finally slowing, standing in front of the Villa Pensa, looking across the street. His tired eyes followed her glance. Ferrara's. How large it had become. She crossed in the middle of the street, not bothering about the desultory traffic, and strolled under the Pasticceria sign into the store.

Nino waited for the light to change and dragged himself across the street. How flashy Ferrara's had gotten. The window was full of packaged boxed candies with fancy Ferrara labels; coffee cans in red and green blared the name again. Sleek display cases showed the pastries. Shiny black-lacquer ice cream parlor chairs; yellow formica tables. Where were the little wooden chairs, the chipped Carrara marble tables, the cozy friendliness of the old place with its trays of pastries? The young waiters, each trying to look like Valentino, had waltzed them around when they felt like it. He leaned against the window and felt its coolness. Now there was even air conditioning. He could see her at a table near the door, ordering. Dizziness and exhaustion rolled over him in waves. His good leg was throbbing horribly, pain working itself up from his toes, through his arch, past the ankle ringed with popping blue veins.

"Come and have some iced coffee," Gina said, reaching uncertainly for his arm. How could she have done it, she thought, looking at his thin hair matted with sweat, the lines deepening in his face, the heightened color in cheeks that seemed to burn with fever. She began to feel remorse. No, she couldn't be drawn that way into regret. If she didn't harden herself against him, she would always be bound to him. She had had her revenge. It wasn't sweet; but it had made the point, all the same.

Nino, sunk in his dizziness, looked at her without recognition, or even, for a moment, surprise. Leaning on her arm, he moved with her into the coolness, the dry frigid air sending a shiver through his body, shocking him into humiliation and sorrow.

"What's this?" he asked, sitting at the chair she held out for him.

"Iced expresso. Better than amphetamines," she joked, adding cream to her huge goblet filled with coffee. "All you have to do is sip, and it sends"—she groped—"a rush of energy into your veins."

She was looking at him steadily, her clear dark eyes probing his. When had she seen him? he wondered. How long had she known he was following her? It was incredible.

"I'm always willing to try something new," he said, aiming for a casual tone. He took a long drink. The black coffee, slightly bitter, smoothed the lump in his throat. The coolness of the place was steadying. To be cool! That it should seem like such a luxury to sit down, to rest, to drink. He should throw it in her face for humiliating him like this. She knew he had nearly killed himself for her; because of her he was dizzy, weak. The waiter was putting another iced coffee in front of him. She must have signaled for it. How self-possessed she was, the little bitch. He watched her, adding sugar and cream to the coffee.

"Why don't you save yourself the trouble and just order coffee ice cream?" he asked her mildly.

"This way it comes out just the way I want," Gina said. The waiter brought them two sfogliatelli. She was really doing it up, he thought. He should crack her across the face with his cane. It would serve her right! But you only did that to a girl her age for one reason, and he wasn't about to do that in public. Not in this neighborhood, where everyone would know what it meant.

I've got him now, Gina thought. He looked awful. It ought to teach him a lesson, not to try to follow me. It was one thing to demand you acted a certain way at home. It was his, after all, rotten as it was. But quite another to think you could dictate everything else. It was a question of freedom. She hated him when he was dictatorial; but now she realized she found him more troublesome when he was pathetic. Since she felt she had won, she was prepared to be kind. Up to a point.

"What a coincidence that we decided to go for a walk in the same place at the same time," Gina said, smiling sweetly and touching his hand.

"Not really," Nino said smoothly. "You've already made it clear it was no coincidence at all."

He was turning it all around; never say die, Nino, right? Her resolve against him was so saturated with shame and wariness it was rapidly retreating to diplomacy. "I was looking for Columbus Park," she lied.

"But you didn't find it," he pointed out.

"No," she agreed. "I didn't."

"You didn't find it because it isn't here," he pointed out. "It's been west and south of here—between Baxter and Mulberry—since the 1890s, when they leveled the ragpicker settlement to build it." My God, would she have been willing to walk all the way past Canal?

"Amazing how many slums and cemeteries have been turned into parks," she choked out.

"Amazing how many parks are turning into slums and cemeteries," he countered.

"Oh, sure. It's one big burial ground." So he wasn't willing to give up. What a dope she had been to think he might.

"Not really," he said. "Not really. What makes you say that? Do you feel ready to go? Is this your idea of putting your life in order?"

She ignored him and sipped her coffee.

"Where were you going?" he demanded softly, gripping her arm.

Gina tightened her face into a smile. "It's just what you said, Nino. I was just going out with you, in my own way." She looked him in the eye.

He looked at her coldly. The enormity of her gall was hard to take in. To think that she could do this to him—drag him around by the nose, and then, when he was exhausted, humiliate him with kindness! She was forcing his hand. He shook his head. If she could do this, she could do anything. He would have to assume that she had. He had no choice.

"Finish your pastry," he ordered. "It's time to go."

"Go where? You're not going to run my life."

"Home," Nino said. "I've had enough walking." He signaled for the check and paid it. "Thanks for your hospitality." He grinned.

He held the door open, ushering her into the street. The thickening evening air, rising from the hot street in steamy fumes, enfolded them.

It had been a perfect morning, Alex thought, running his nails through Gina's hair as he stretched beside her under the light sheet. In his mind he could see the cables of the bridge, the walkway rising out of the steaming traffic, the wind coming up, blowing the noise away. On the Brooklyn Bridge, the wooden walkway climbed above the traffic, suspended, separate, hanging. If you looked down, you could see the water shimmering between the slats of wood. The moving cars were a blur of color. In the distance the ferries to Staten Island came and went, looking like the round-bottomed ships of a hundred years before. Governor's Island faced them; beyond it, to the right, stood the Statue of Liberty. The sunlight glinted and shone on the river. The hot wind whipped the whitecaps, and blew through the cables crisscrossing toward the arches.

She had been restless all the while. He had motioned her to a bench, but she wouldn't sit down; she kept reaching in all directions, her tense hands curling around the cables as if she were ready to climb. She probably believes she can fly. The truth was, her energy often irritated him. She could fly over his moods as though they didn't exist. She always seemed to have an unswervable, hidden purpose of her own. They had been lovers for weeks now, and she had never asked him anything much about himself. Not that she talked about herself. It wasn't that she was selfish; she wasn't. But there were things you could say to her and things you couldn't. She doesn't think about herself, but she doesn't think about me, either, he concluded. She reminded him of one of these mafiosi who takes you to lunch, tells you sincerely that he holds you in the highest regard, and apologizes that there's nothing personal in it when he shoots you before dessert. She loved him, he could see that, but there didn't seem to be anything personal in it.

On the bridge she hadn't seemed to know he was there. She was revved up on the heat and light, on whatever it was that made her reach so steadily outside herself. Then, in bed, touching him, she would be so filled with everything, she would confuse him with her exaltation. She was so loving it was hard to be annoyed. Maybe I'm better off that she doesn't ask what I feel. She doesn't know my problems, my lows. She has no idea who I am. Hades one-upped because Persephone mistakes him for a fellow flower picker.

Gina turned toward him, and smiled, as she rolled up on top of him. She began to kiss his chest, nuzzling softly into him as she caressed his body. In the distance, he could see the luminous clock hands showing a yellow-green 8:00 P.M. as they brightened in the darkening room.

When Gina didn't get home by seven, Nino and Laura decided to get on the BMT. They got off at Union Square and walked for a block; then, convinced they would never make it on foot to Avenue D, Laura hailed a cab. The whole neighborhood had changed.

"You don't want to go there," said the old cab driver. "It's not the same neighborhood."

"I have to go there," Nino said, consulting the note he had made of Alex's address. At the Motor Vehicle Bureau they had records you could trust. Now he even knew his age: twenty-six. He gnashed his teeth.

"You better be careful," the driver said, watching him limp out of the cab with Laura behind him. "Old people are a big target here."

"That's right," Nino said. "The old and the young get it first."

They got lost in two alleys before they found his apartment.

"It's not even a tenement," Nino said.

"It's the worst place I've ever seen," said Laura. "Is that the door?"

Nino hesitated, trying to decide whether he should knock with his cane or his fist. He pounded the door with his fist.

"Don't answer it," Gina whispered to Alex.

"Why not?" asked Alex. "It's probably Kevin. I want you to meet him."

"I just have a bad feeling," she insisted. "Would Kevin bang on the door like that?"

Alex shrugged.

"Let me get dressed first," Gina said, reaching for her skirt.

"Here, take this," said Alex, throwing her the silky orange kimono he had bought her.

She tied it as he pulled on his pants and called, "Just a minute."

When he opened the door, Nino and Laura ignored him. "I thought you'd be here," Nino said. Gina clutched the kimono around her as his cane whacked across her shoulders. "Get your clothes on," he said. Alex took a step toward her, but stopped. She turned to him, humiliation sweeping over her like a sandstorm.

"These are your parents?" Alex said to her. "You'd better get dressed."

It was all collapsing, the sense of privacy, safety, freedom, all falling in. She squeezed into the tiny bathroom with her clothes.

"You've taken advantage of my daughter," Laura sobbed.

"I'm not taking advantage of anyone," he said. "I haven't forced her to come here. She wants to be here."

"Watch what you say," Nino said. "Remember, you're in trouble enough as it is."

"What would your parents say if they knew? Do you think your parents would approve of this?"

"Why don't you ask them?" he said, dialing a number. He handed the telephone to Laura, who became totally disconcerted.

His father answered.

"My name," Laura said uncertainly, "is Laura. Your son . . . I'm in your son's apartment and I discovered him here with my daughter. He's taken advantage of her — she's very young . . ." Laura began to cry. "No, I don't think he's used physical force. But he's taken advantage of her all the same. . . . If she wants to be here, it's because he's made her want to be here. . . . What do you mean, what do I expect you to do? I expect you to stop him. . . . You have no business telling me that. Don't you know right from wrong? Haven't you got any morals?"

She turned, still holding the phone. "He says if she wants to be here, there's nothing any of us can do about it and then he hung up."

"Like father, like son," Nino agreed.

"You," he said to Gina as she came out, dressed, "you get out in the hallway. It would serve you right if you got bitten by the rats. And you," he said, poking Alex with his cane, "I'm not finished with you. In fact, I haven't even started." He nodded to Laura to leave and began to walk out. Gina came back into the room to see Alex. He turned away from her. "You'd better go," he said. "All of you."

They walked through the dark alleyway and turned on Avenue D toward Fourteenth Street. In the darkness, the slight movements of cats through garbage cans, the breeze ruffling newspapers, the crackle of wrappers tumbling down the street seemed like explosions. They were going off like grenades in Gina's brain. She couldn't stop seeing Alex turn from her; the angle of his head, his dismissal. The scene kept playing before her eyes. He had been glad to get rid of all of them.

"So this was the point of taking me to lunch," she said to Nino. "This was why you came to the office."

"So you can still talk," Nino said. "I found out his name."

"Why didn't you just ask me? If you had just asked me, I would have told you."

"Why should I think you would tell me if you hadn't

before? Why did you hide him?" he hissed. "Are you ashamed of him? You ought to be. What's he hiding behind that beard? Why didn't you bring him to the house?"

"Because I know how you hate everyone who isn't exactly like you. I didn't want you to spoil it for me, the way you have now."

"I spoil it for *you!* You're the one who spoiled your life. You have the judgment of an idiot! You expect me to approve of my own daughter becoming a whore?"

"Nino, be quiet," Laura said. "Wait until we get home."

"If you gave him a chance, you would have liked him. He's very decent."

"Decent!"

"He may not be like you," she said, "but he . . . has been good to me. People do things differently now. This isn't Sicily."

"Don't mention Sicily to me. In Sicily you wouldn't be alive."

"If his not coming to the house is an issue, he will come to the house."

"The fact that he didn't insist on meeting your family shows he doesn't take you seriously. The fact that you didn't insist shows you're a fool. I could have looked him over and told you he was no good. You don't have to ask someone like that his intentions," Nino concluded, "because you already know what they are."

Gina groaned. She couldn't say what her own intentions were, much less his. Nino was great at ruining things by pushing them to a crisis, forcing you to make choices. It was like running a race in which the hurdles were raised and raised until you finally tripped. No matter how much you practiced and trained, you could never win because the hurdles would always loom higher and higher. It taught you your limitations, gave you a sense of the boundaries of your feelings. Would you marry him? Would you spend the rest of your life with him? The questions, raising the prospect of eternity with Alex, were making her realize how little she wanted anyone "forever." What about Alex's intentions? He wants to "improve" me, she thought wryly. To play Svengali to my Trilby, Pygmalion to my Galatea. He wants to free me from the burden of my working-class practicality. He wants to show me that the only thing that matters is having a good time, now. Nino had certainly loused that up for tonight.

She could see how wounded Nino was by the sight of her in Alex's place. Well, he brought it on himself by going there.

"You don't know what his intentions are," she said. "You don't know him at all. Give him a chance. He never came to the house because I wouldn't let him. Despite what you think, nothing happened between us."

Nino stared at her. "Because I don't have a good leg, it doesn't mean I don't have one to stand on. If you're lucky, nothing irreversible happened. If it did, I warn you," he said, lifting his cane and resting it against the right side of her face, "you'll have to keep it, raise it. You won't get a dime from me to do it. Then maybe you'll learn your lesson."

"You have nothing to worry about," she said, pushing his cane away, but actually it was the first time it had occurred to her that she did.

"You have no shame," he said. "Look at you." Her face was dead white. "You're pretty calm. You don't feel affected. You talk, but you forget what to say, how to apologize, how to repent for sneaking around."

"It's an open question which one of us is more of a sneak," she said evenly.

"I'm your father," he said. "It's my job."

When they reached Union Square she hesitated at the edge of the subway stairs. If she turned and ran, she could go back. He would want her back, alone.

"Hurry up," said Nino, banging his cane on the sidewalk. "Do you think I'm going to take a cab? I've already spent more than you're worth tonight."

She stiffened. It was easier to hate him than to feel humiliated by him. Nino had hurt her, but not as badly as Alex. He had been upset by her parents' barging in. How could he not be? But she had been shocked by his look of pettish disgust. He had behaved as though she and Nino and Laura were droning insects who had startled him out of a sound sleep and driven him to retreat under his covers. There was something cowardly in his air of being too fastidious to deal with them. Dialing his father, getting rid of her along with them—he had taken the easy way out.

She had never put into words what she saw in Alex. Initially she had been attracted to him because he seemed so polished and yet so relaxed and amused. He had a kind of self-assurance she hadn't seen in anyone before. He was older than she, but that wasn't it. He had an aloof superiority that wasn't connected with anything real, like money or possessions or achievements. It was an air of knowingness, of being part of an elect who knew it all and never had to get upset. Nino was always upset about something.

Alex never sweated for anything. Yet he could work meticulously at his Chinese. He had majored in mathematics, but had never gotten his degree. He didn't need to know Chinese to be a mathematician. The difficulty of the language seemed to make it all the more important to him. She loved to watch him work on his ideographs. Yet she noticed that with all his apparent interest, he was still working on the same chapter, perhaps even the same page. A lot of what he did seemed to have become an end in itself, a diversionary tactic to ward off the finality of a decision about what to do with his life.

I'm being hard on him because he hurt me, Gina thought.

I care for him because he is always interesting to me. He made me realize how lonely I was. She had always had friends, but never anyone who could unleash such intense feelings of joy and intimacy. Sometimes, with other girls, she could talk about going to school. Her friend, Nancy, was brilliant, but even worse off than she. Her father worked hard, but there were nine kids in the family and all the boys would get to go to college before she would. She had wanted to be a doctor, but had won a scholarship to nursing school and had taken it, just to get away.

Gina had always felt like something of a misfit among the other girls. They could talk about makeup and clothes or even books or people, but then would come the moments when they would make quick and easy confessions to each other that seemed to be the cement between them. She had lots of weaknesses to confess, but she could never talk, could never make a show of her helplessness. When her friends came up to commiserate with her after Nino had brought that rejection letter to school, she had politely rebuffed them. Was it pride or fear? She had too much of both. She had seen them confide only to regret it when their confidantes talked, talked, talked. She was too much like Nino—imposing absurd standards of conduct nobody met, digging in behind them and finding nothing but isolation.

They had reached the subway platform. The sight of it made her want to turn and run back to Alex. She couldn't. Not tonight. The idea of escaping from Nino began to flicker in the back of her mind. What could she say to him now? Should there be an open confrontation, no lying, just a statement that Alex was what she wanted? If she were a man, it would have been easier. Nino respected physical power. He would have condemned a man for fooling around with a "nice" girl, but he would have understood. Her being a woman triggered emotions of protectiveness and honor that sprang out of a dim Sicilian past. That was it, she thought. For Nino the loss of honor had less to do with her than with a judgment on him. It was his vanity that was at stake. He needed to be so respected that nobody would mess with his daughter.

She and Alex had not paid him the respect he thought he deserved. He had sent out his bill of obligations due. And now he wanted it paid in the coin of sentiment and right behavior: apologies, marriage, everlasting repentance. She would never be able to meet his price. He had come to foreclose on her freedom. Father, daughter, lover—they all seemed cast into the roles of an Italian opera. She was determined that no one should die in the last act. Especially she herself.

Nino was bent on getting what was due him. Maybe she could meet his demands, up to a point.

"Let me ask if we could compromise," Gina said to Nino in a conciliatory tone.

"You aren't in a position to bargain for anything," he answered. But she could see his curiosity was piqued.

"I'll have him come to the house and you can talk to him. Until then, in return, you do nothing."

"And you?" Nino demanded. "What do you do?"

Gina shrugged noncommittally.

"That's reasonable," Laura said quickly. "Until we find out what the situation is, it pays to do that. We may," she said softly, "need him to . . . you . . . if she . . ." her voice trailed off. When the train reached their stop, none of them had a word to say. They walked home slowly, keeping pace with Nino's limp. When they got home, all his rage seemed to have drained into exhaustion. Nino sat down.

"I can't think anymore tonight," he said. "Get out of my sight," he said to Gina. "I'll tell you what I intend to do with you in the morning."

She walked into her room. Laura came in behind her. Sitting numbly on the bed, she looked at her mother. Her eyes began to burn.

"How could you do this?" Laura said. "Didn't I always give you the best advice?"

"I took it. You always said, 'Never marry a Sicilian.' So I didn't. I haven't." Gina looked at her mother. Her eyes filled with tears. *I know why he does this. But not you. Not you.*

"This time," Laura said, looking at the floor, "he's right. This is the right thing to do." She reached out to smooth Gina's hair, but Gina moved out of reach.

Gina sat, waiting for her to leave. When she did, Gina pressed her face into the pillow, trying to bury her revulsion and pain. But it was there waiting for her when Nino banged on her door the next morning. "You," he said, knocking open the door, "invite him to dinner. We'll see what he is."

She looked at him. She felt embalmed, but picked up the telephone and did what he asked. Alex was curt but agreed to come for coffee. "Dinner," he explained, "will be too long. I'll speak to your father, then maybe we can take a walk."

It was only eight o'clock in the morning, but it was already 91 in the shade. She stayed in her room, so that Nino would have to come in and ask her if Alex was coming. When she said yes, he nodded and locked her in her room. It was when she heard the lock turn that she made up her mind to get away. *I can climb out the window,* she thought at first. *It was just a few feet from the ground.* But then there was too much still unplanned. Tomorrow she would register for school at Hunter College. She would need a place to stay. Fear welled up around the thoughts of escape, but somehow making plans forced it back until even the fear was a kind of encouragement. Outside, the wet heat seemed to whiten as the day went on. In the dim, shaded room where the sun never reached, she figured and slept. When she woke, her sheets were wet with blood. Rolling them into a ball, she smiled. Her mood seemed to lighten; her freedom seemed to surge with the streaming blood.

Forgetting Nino had locked the door, she tried it. It was open and he had gone. She ran a bath and rinsed the sheets in the sink before throwing them in the washing machine. It was all coming together, she thought. Her luck! Had it been waiting for her there, someplace unknown, before now? She would never leave anything to chance again. But she had touched it, her luck, at last. Her belly felt flat and warm. Everything was working. Maybe it would always work, maybe she could always feel this sense of possessing and repossessing herself, of retrieving herself. The thought of leaving home made her feel better and better. She thought of discussing it with Alex, but he would assume she was leaving for him. He'd probably be afraid she wanted to live with him. She didn't. She would plan her escape herself.

Her desk was still cluttered with last term's reading. She began to arrange things for her big move. She picked up her books and sorted them into stacks. *Hero with a Thousand Faces*; *The Myth of the Eternal Return*; *Into Eden: American Puritanism*. That book had led to her first conversation with Alex. She had read it for a course and decided to finish it over the summer. Alex had seen it on her desk and told her his father had written it. She had been even more impressed when she learned that his father had come from a down-and-out Ohio family and, after his success as a historian, had become cultural advisor to the American embassy in Paris. Not bad for a poor farm boy.

There was a kind of redemption in escaping the place where you were born, the limits of the world around you. Even just reading multiplied environments because you could, at least for a while, live in the world of the book. What she loved about anthropology was the mass of possible worlds it offered. The concrete problems of life were deadeningly repetitive, but the immense variety of cultural solutions was dazzling. Why did she have to live the way Nino lived or think the way Nino thought? She began to hum. She was tired of thinking about her own feelings. Anthropology and history took your mind off emotions. She was anxious to get back to school.

Alex arrived with bouquets of lilac and mimosa. He gave one to Laura, who took it into the kitchen and started to cry. The mimosa was for Gina, who just held it and looked at him. He was very elegant in a heavy woolen suit with a vest, a pale blue shirt, and a silk tie. From the sofa where he sat with his bad leg elevated, Nino watched him too.

"It's interesting that you can wear a suit like that this time of year without sweating," Nino said. He was enjoying this more than he had expected.

"It seemed appropriate to wear a suit, Mr. Giardello, and this is the only one I have," Alex said, and smiled.

"Sit down, sit down. Have some coffee," Nino said as Laura returned with a pot of espresso. "Take off your jacket. After all, we're practically related."

Alex sat down, slightly disconcerted. He did not remove his jacket. Gina stood in the doorway, watching.

"You know," Nino continued, "we're an interesting family. Gina's cousin—she must have told you about him. He is an excellent marksman. He's in the Army now, but still active in the National Rifle Association."

"I'm not much for violence," said Alex.

"Among friends, violence is never necessary," Nino agreed. "Of course, none of us is for violence. However, sometimes," he shrugged, "there is no other way."

Laura had begun to pray to Saint Anthony. Gina could tell by the angle of her eyes.

"Where are you from?" Nino asked, beginning in earnest.

"Amsterdam, I was born in Amsterdam," Alex said. "Then I lived in Paris. I came here when I was six."

"Ah," Nino said. "An immigrant."

Alex looked at him. "You might say. My father was working in Europe."

"What do you do besides working as a stamp perforator?"

"I have a leave of absence from Brown. After three years, I wanted some time off."

"Backed out just before the end? If you wanted to get away, why did you hang around a school?"

Alex shrugged.

"What were you studying?"

"Mathematics and chemistry."

"Chemistry," Nino said. "Now that's a good subject. Well, did you flunk out? Were you about to flunk out?"

"No," said Alex. "I did very well. I went to Stuyvesant. I did all right," he said lamely.

"So the reason you quit was something else."

"I was uncertain what I wanted to do, or whether I wanted to stay there. I heard the opportunities might be better out west and thought I might finish there."

"So you are confused. You thought to better yourself and in the process you did nothing. Confusion," Nino said, "is a bad business. Perhaps I can help you. You don't have to be confused anymore." Nino tapped him on the chest. "When you're in trouble, you know exactly where you are."

Alex stared at him. Finally he recovered himself enough to say, "There is no reason for me to think I'm in trouble. I wouldn't be troubled by marrying your daughter, if that's what you're concerned about. I'll marry her."

There was an audible intake of breath from Laura which Nino ignored. Gina felt as though she were watching an ancient ritual of sacrifice. She and Alex were the offerings, but also the reasons for each other's victimization. Each of them was being used to trap the other. Nino was in his element. She could see that he was pleased at how it was going and had sensed that Alex could be made to do whatever he wanted.

"Have some of this," Nino said, almost smiling as he poured anisette into an empty water glass and handed it to Alex. He waited for Alex to taste it before he poured some into his own black coffee and took a long drink.

"One month should be enough time to make all the arrangements," Nino said genially. "We don't have to settle the details tonight."

"What do you know about baseball?" Nino asked.

"Nothing," Alex answered.

"I thought so," Nino said. "I've been a Yankee fan since 1935."

"It's getting late," Alex said. "May I take Gina for a walk?"

Nino looked at Laura. Everyone in the neighborhood would know. But if they were going to get married, they would know anyway. Finally Nino said, "A short walk is OK. Turn left immediately as you leave the house."

"Why?" Alex said.

"Because that's the right way to walk," Nino said.

Alex nodded and rose from his chair. "It was nice to have met you," he said, extending his hand. Nino shook it. "Thank you for the coffee, Mrs. Giardello," he said to Laura.

"You're very welcome," Laura said.

Alex began walking down the long hall. Its uneven floor, lumpy walls cluttered with yellowed pictures, and lack of natural light suggested catacombs for the living dead. Her father's questioning was bad enough, but the cramped ugliness of the place was repulsive. How could they stand it?

Gina could see how Alex had taken it in. She had never liked the living room, but she had been able to shut it out except as a too-crowded alcove on the way to her room. Now she saw that the gray-beige paint Nino had chosen was so grim it must have looked aged even while it was being applied. The paltriness of the room came down on her. The new fluted silk lamp shades had plastic shrouds, the green sofa lay under its vinyl-backed throw, the heavy wooden table with its linen cloth was covered by clear plastic—even the furniture was suffocating. The huge table filled the center of the room, leaving barely enough space to edge around it to the chairs. After dinner it could be pushed into place against the wall, baring the honey-colored floors Laura carefully scrubbed and waxed, scarred despite all her care by chairs being pushed back from the table. She knew Alex had seen it that way. It was best to say nothing.

Gina followed Alex quickly out of the apartment, leaving without a word. On the street, he turned to her and asked, "I think I did OK, don't you?"

"You were great," she said. How could he know that nothing he did or didn't do would have made a difference? "You look terrific in a suit."

"It's too hot, but I thought it would impress them," he said simply. The sound of thunder rumbled through the thick, hot air.

"I'm sure it did," she said, wanting to take his hand. But she wouldn't until they made their way past the neighbors her mother always called "the brigade." There they were— Mrs. Di Costa in black twenty years after the death of her husband, Mrs. Cerisi mourning the son lost in World War II. Her daughter, Mrs. Picci, was there in black for the husband shot in Korea. They were the mothers and grand-mothers of the kids who played in the yard. Every time she saw them, they seemed to spell out the succession of weddings, births, funerals, visits to the sick and dying, appearances at wakes. One wake after the other until finally you yourself were the main attraction, the guest of honor. To the right they stretched on, more neighbors looking for a breeze in the heat. To the left there were private houses where no one sat outside. They turned left, avoiding the gossipy super's wife Laura called "the radio."

Alex took off his jacket and threw it over one shoulder. "Your father is a riot," he said, shaking his head. " 'When you're in trouble, you know exactly where you are.' Too much! and 'What do you know about baseball?' " Alex laughed.

Gina gave him a hard look.

"Well, I mean they're old-fashioned and worried about you. It'll be all right now. I think they'll leave us alone."

"Nino won't leave us alone," Gina said.

"Why not? Did he mean that about getting married?" Alex asked.

"Do you mean *you* didn't mean it?" Gina asked him pointedly.

"I don't know. I never thought about it."

"You just agreed to marry me in a month," Gina said. "Aren't you aware of that."

"We were just talking. In a way, it was funny being looked over. Nobody ever did that to me before. Do you want to get married?" Alex asked, wondering if she had put the old man up to this.

"Do you think I do?" Gina asked.

"I don't know. I haven't figured you out yet. If it's that important to you, I guess we could do it," Alex said.

He probably would marry her if she pressed him, but that didn't mean he would behave any differently than if he were single. She suspected that, either way, he would turn Nino into the stuff of anecdotes. He didn't take anything seriously, she realized.

"I could never accept a deal Nino had made," Gina said softly.

"Don't look at it that way," Alex said. "We only agreed in principle. We never got to the details." He started to laugh. He put his arms around her, and pulled her toward him. "Now that we're engaged, we can do it solemnly." He laughed, kissing her.

"I have to get back," she said, laughing despite her turmoil.

"I'll take you home," he offered.

"No, I'd rather you didn't," she answered. She could see the two of them running the gauntlet of staring women in perpetual black. They parted without touching at the station. The thunder sounded closer now.

When she came back she found her mother stuffing lilacs into a garbage bag.

"How could you do it?" Laura asked. "I still can't understand it."

"Do what? Look, it's not as though I'm pregnant. I haven't done anything. He was very polite to you." She retrieved a branch from the garbage bag. "I'm hot and I have my period," she said. "Just leave me alone about it. I can't go through life doing only what you tell me."

"If you would only listen to me. Arthur would make such a good husband. He's loyal, hard-working, and he isn't Sicilian," Laura whispered.

"Neither is Alex."

"He's too peculiar. You'll never know what he thinks. Besides, just listening to him, you can see he has no future. Not to mention that he's strange."

Gina went into her room, but Laura was determined to continue and followed her in.

"He thought you might accept him because he was so polite despite what Dad did."

"What did your father do? He just told the truth. If he thinks we would accept him, that proves he has no sense of reality. Listen to me. You're not pregnant. Thank God! This isn't Sicily. No one has to know this. Just forget about him. I promise that I won't let your father make you marry him. I swear it," Laura pleaded.

Gina said nothing. Laura waited until it was clear there was no reason to think waiting would do any good.

Alone, Gina undressed for bed. She could hear Laura and Nino talking in the living room, but could not make out what they were saying. The evening had been a disaster. Not a run-of-the-mill disaster, but a debacle. Still, the thought of Alex made her smile. She was tired of heavy feelings and grim moods.

She was in a deep sleep when Nino pounded at her door and barged in. He stood over her, enraged. "You're never to see or talk to him again," he said. "Understand?" he demanded. He raised his cane as if to hit her, but caught himself and, instead, swept it across the surface of her desk, knocking her neat piles of books and papers to the floor. "It's finished. This time you're getting off easy, but I intend to make sure there is no next time. This is the end. Just accept that, and don't try to talk your way out of it."

She stared at him in silence.

"Just remember, you go to school, you cut him out of your mind. He's an idiot."

"He was willing to marry me. Wasn't that what you wanted?"

"You think I wanted you to marry the kind of man who would marry a woman he already knew was a whore?" Nino said. His words roused him to look for something else to knock over and he waved his cane.

"Don't do that!" Gina cried, catching the end of the cane and holding it fast.

Nino looked at her, startled.

"You made your point. You got what you said you wanted. Isn't that enough for one night? Do you have to stage a terrorist raid, too?"

The quiet, even fury in her voice chilled him.

"You've humiliated me, pushed me around, destroyed something that meant a lot to me. Isn't that enough?"

"Someday you'll thank me for destroying it," Nino said quietly.

Gina let go of his cane. "Don't bet on it."

Nino leaned toward her. "Someday *he'll* thank me for destroying it. You have no heart. You're all ice and steel."

"My heart be—longs to Dad—dy, Da—da—da, Da—da—dad—dy," Gina sang with a malicious smile.

"That'll be the day," Nino said, his face darkening with sorrow. He turned to leave the room, pausing to knock the stacked papers from the top of her bookcase. "Just remember, this is the end of it." He slammed the door behind him.

She felt trapped in the shambles he had made of her room. The walls seemed to move in; even the alley outside the narrow window seemed part of a prison. Always the sense of suffocation that felt like an emptying out of life, a loss of will as well as air. It was too narcotizing to be painful; too terrible, too dreary, too familiar to tolerate anymore. Why not simply leave? It wasn't only for Alex. There were lots of times when even he got on her nerves, when his humor seemed only deceptive or just too precious for her. What drew her to him, in a way, was Nino.

Nino made everything so rough, so bleak, so guarded, that the craving for color, for softness, was overpowering. She would give anything to be out of here, and—why not?—in Alex's whitewashed room, feeling his touch and the light hair on his back, the sun gleaming on his body. . . . Should she live with him? Just move in? That would be one way. And even that would be better than staying here. This was the place of old humiliations and failures. How many nightmares had there been of planes crashing, of sleek, fast-moving trains suddenly derailing, falling into space and flames. Here she would always have nightmares that narrowed everything to death or mutilation or worse: the fear, coming again and again in dreams, of being paralyzed from the neck down, unable either to die or live. It was these that frightened her more than anything, more than Nino. They say you make your own nightmares; you can have them turn out any way at all. But these fearful dreams flourished only here. They grew in Nino's house like living plaster, sealing everything into grim stability.

Yet something was giving way. Even the heat seemed to be breaking. She could hear thunder cracking high overhead; lightning flashed sharply on the wall outside. The rain would come, finishing off the heat that had lingered into September. She scooped papers from the floor, crumpled them into a ball, and threw it against the wall. She had to find a place where she could breathe.

Four

The Bristol Residence Hotel wasn't exactly a place to live. What people did there was mill around. Some drifted in and out, renting by the week. Some stayed until they could find apartments or roommates. Only the edgy winos and muttering recluses were hard-core regulars. She knew Kevin, Alex's best friend, lived there with his pretty blonde girlfriend, Molly, who was just her age. Gina had met them the week before when Kevin had come into the West End bar with a dead roach perched on each shoulder, like epaulets. He was so wound up he scarcely knew where he was; his intense blue eyes, moving restlessly while he talked, seemed to take no notice of Molly. He had been a flier in Japan. He had studied Zen with Suzuki. Stories poured out of him like hot beer.

"I still don't get it," he had told Suzuki. "Explain it again." Suzuki had grabbed his shoulders, shaken him, and banged his head against a wall. "That," Suzuki said, "is the point." He got it, that time. Truth had come to Kevin as a black and blue bump. "Few of us have such certainty," Molly had said dryly, flicking a roach from his left shoulder. Kevin told Zen stories rapid-fire. Gina's favorite was the one where a man comes to Master Joshu crying, "Master, I have nothing!" "You have nothing?" Joshu repeated. "Throw it away!"

The way in, Gina thought, walking into the Bristol, is the way out. The place didn't have what you could call a service desk. It had a massive switchboard run by a Belgian named Gerard, who had been a graduate student at Columbia for sixteen years. The board flashed lights and buzzed. Some calls Gerard connected; others he didn't. How, she wondered, did he decide which?

"Is there anyone around who can tell me if any rooms are available?" she asked.

"I'm it," Gerard said, "I'm the staff. There are a few." He picked up a gray cardboard, the kind laundries wrap shirts around. On it were scribbled room numbers, crossed-out dates, and little notes. "One big corner room with a smaller one behind it for twenty-five a week. Then there's a large single room for twenty. Community kitchen and bathroom," he added, squinting at the cardboard.

The thought of sharing a bathtub with the unknown made her flinch. "Are there any rooms with baths?" she asked.

"Just one left. It's very small. Just a maid's room for twelve twenty-five a week. It's really small," he repeated, ignoring the buzzes and lights on the board.

"I'd like to see it anyway," she said. "Can I leave my suitcase here?"

He nodded, took off the headphones dangling around his neck, and walked toward the back to lock up her bag. When he saw her looking at the board, he shrugged. "If it's really important, they'll call back. Maybe when they do, I'll be here. If I'm here, maybe I'll plug in the call."

They took the smelly elevator to the twelfth floor. He was right. The room was small, about five feet wide, except for an alcove just big enough for a single bed. By stretching her arms, she could touch both sides of the room. It was painted battleship gray and had a big window overlooking the roofs of the lower buildings on 113th Street. A closet, narrow table, a beat-up wooden chair, and a small, scarred chest of drawers crowded the tiny room. The bathroom, on the other hand, was enormous. A huge old tub with lion's foot legs, a stained oval sink, and a toilet, all set into cracked white tile. Between the cracks, amazingly, little weeds grew.

"I'll take it," she said.

"OK," Gerard said. "You have to pay in advance and fill out a card." Gina went back down to the switchboard, filled out her name, but not her previous address, and paid for the week. He began to plug in some calls. She picked up the key he pushed toward her and went back up to the room alone. She sat down on the bed.

She would have liked to pace the room, but there wasn't any room to pace. She went to the window and sat on the sill. The roofs are lovely, she thought, looking at the irregular line of vents, the skylights of the old brownstones in the middle of the block, the soft gray cement facings on the backs of the buildings.

She saw something move on the roof below. She looked down more carefully and made out a cat slinking stealthily against the base of a skylight. A few feet from him was a small, bright orange bird. The bird was wobbling on its feet. The cat paused, its eyes fixed on the bird. Sensing something wrong, the bird began hopping frantically and trying to fly. Its wings must be damaged, Gina thought. The cat drew back, lunged, and pounced. A few feathers flying loose from his claws were all that was left of the bird. The cat licked his paws and stretched in the sun.

Another power struggle, Gina thought, but more sickening and raw than mine. It was impossible to love the cat, but no one would want to be the bird. She had gotten out before Nino could pounce. Today she had won. But there had to be something better, some life somewhere that wasn't full of power plays, struggles for control. Still, that was the world she lived in. If she lost her balance Nino would be there, seizing the opportunity to strike. She had to keep steady. She could do it. Hunter was cheap. She had worked after school and summers since her second year in high school and had already saved enough tuition money to finish the two years she had to go. She loved studying anthropology. She had two job prospects—word-processing for a midtown law firm or a marketing research company. Both paid more than the job she had now. One or the other would come through. Small assets, but big enough to help her survive and graduate without loans or debts or Nino. So much for the good side. There were weaknesses too, she realized, unable to take her eyes off the cat. One of them was Alex. He was bad for game plans. Her longing for him sometimes frightened her. It was extravagant, out of control. That's what's wonderful about it, she thought. She was sick of being wary, careful.

She moved away from the window. "I'm not the cat and I'm not the bird. I will not be the bird. Here I am, whatever I am," Gina murmured. She ran her fingers along the wall, trying to take it all in. Tension seemed to flow away from her. "I'm home," she announced to herself.

She unpacked her bag, and when everything was in order, left, locking the door behind her. At the end of the corridor was a pay telephone. Next to it was a sign: "Answer the phone and yell who it's for!" So this is the tenants' answer to Gerard, she thought, dropping in a coin. She waited excitedly while it rang, eager to tell Alex what she had done. But he wasn't there. She took the stinking elevator down, too excited to stay in her room.

She walked down Broadway, browsing in stores, looking at

the people on the street moving purposefully along or just hanging out. At Ninety-sixth Street, she realized there was no real reason for her to be anywhere. No one expected her anywhere. By now Nino and Laura would have gotten her note. They would know she wasn't coming back. She was free. She sat down on a bench in the late sunlight, ignoring the bag lady at the end of the bench, scarcely noticing the traffic bellowing fumes. A vendor stood, waiting to cross the rest of the street. He was selling buttons. She read them: Kiss me, I'm Polish! A Woman's Place Is in the House and Senate. Near the bottom was a blue and white one that said Stamp Out Reality.

"I'll take that one," she said, pointing to it. Stamp Out Reality. There's a cause, she thought, handing him a quarter. A man sat down and began to speak to her in a low voice in Spanish. She looked at him and turned away. After a while he left and she went back to dreaming. Why shouldn't it be all over? Why can't you stamp it out? She could still hear Nino saying, When you leave the old ways you know what you will lose, but not what you will find. Stamp them all out anyway, she decided. So long as I lose them, I don't care what I find. Anyway, I don't want to know in advance. If I could imagine what would happen—it hit her—it wouldn't be what I wanted. I want something I don't know how to imagine now.

She started walking. By the time she reached Seventy-eighth Street she thought she'd try Alex again. "I'm living at the Bristol," she said cheerfully. "I have this fantastic room with a bath."

There was silence at the other end of the phone.

"Aren't you glad?" she said. "I knew it was the right thing to do."

"If it's what you want," he said cautiously. "Isn't your father going to come after you? Does he know you're there? This time he might bring your cousin with the gun."

Gina stared at the phone. It wasn't like Alex to panic. Or was it?

"Maybe he will; maybe he won't. I don't know. I can't *not* tell them where I am." She intended to mail them her address the next day. She was too curious to see what Alex would do to let him know that now.

There was another silence, and finally Alex said, "I'll call you later."

"Why don't you come over?" she asked.

"Maybe later. I have to think about it."

"OK." Gina tried not to sound disappointed. Somehow she thought they would celebrate. It wasn't so much fun alone. By the time she walked back to the Bristol, she felt hungry. She decided to check out the community kitchen, a dingy, windowless room near the end of the hall. Its turquoise walls peeled back here and there to expose a whitish flaking paper. A sign on the old Philco refrigerator read, EATING SOMEONE ELSE'S FOOD IS STEALING. An old man in an undershirt sat drinking beer at a battered metal table in the corner. There was a vacant chair opposite him. He waved his hand toward it, inviting her to sit down.

"Not just yet," she said, backing toward the door. She would have to get a hot plate for her room. But for tonight, she thought, ringing the elevator, a sandwich and ginger ale would do. She ate on a stone bench, watching the light fade. Somehow, it was dawning on her, it was hard to stay in that room. It meant freedom, and that thought alone kept pushing her out. And it was, maybe, just too gray. On her way back, she bought a plant, a pot of mums the color of cinnamon, rich, rust-orange blossoms, bobbing in all directions. She watched them as she brushed her teeth, changed their position as she brushed her hair, and looked at the stems as she got in bed. She pressed her face to the pillow. No more Nino alarm clocks, she thought. It's all over. And she fell into a deep sleep.

It was Alex who woke her, nuzzling into her cheek. "Princess Persephone," he murmured, climbing on top of her, "you did this for me."

"How did you get in here?" she asked, half irritated. All this so no one could just wake her up, and here he was!

"Gerard let me in. I told him all about everything. I've known him for years. I told Kevin, too. If you need anything, you can count on Kevin."

"I don't need Kevin. What time is it?" she asked.

"I'm not staying," he said, getting up. "What if they come and hurt you and I'm not here," he said.

"So, be here," she said. "You came all the way here, why not stay?"

"No," he said quickly, "this is between you and them."

"If you think I did this for you, isn't it between all of us?"

"I won't be here," Alex repeated, "but I'll call. Have you any money for food?"

She nodded. "Do you want to go out for a drink together? I don't know what time it is," she said, realizing she would have to get an alarm clock.

"No, it wouldn't be a good idea." Alex kissed her cheek and her hand. "Kevin will look out for you. You can rely on him. But stay away from Molly," he added. "She's a troublemaker."

"How can Molly get me into any more trouble than you did?" she asked, smiling at him.

"Oh, you haven't seen anything yet," he said. "I'll call you later." He hesitated and then walked out quickly, locking the door with a key he had somehow managed to get.

She didn't think Nino would come here. He wouldn't want

to face it. He would either send the police, or more likely, think she would fold in a day or so and come home. He might even write me off, she thought hopefully. That would be just like him. The trouble was, what he would or wouldn't do didn't seem to matter to her anymore. It was as if in leaving she had broken the spell. He wasn't very real to her now. Just in the last few hours, she seemed to have begun to see everything from a very great distance. Here is Alex, coming in the middle of the night just to tell her he wasn't going to stay, just to say he was palming her off on Kevin. If he cared, she thought, he would stay himself. It wasn't that he didn't care. It was just that he couldn't do it. He was too weak to go the distance. In some ways, she thought, Nino is right about him. That was the trouble with Nino. He wasn't a fool. So you had to take him seriously.

Chi gioca solo non perde mai—the man who plays alone never loses. When she wasn't around Nino his proverbs seemed bigger signposts than before. She didn't want to think about him; she didn't want to think about Alex. Maybe, she thought, I'll change the lock. But it's too late to do anything now. She tried to go back to sleep, but somehow she couldn't. There was someone nearby with a horrible, explosive cough. Every cough sounded like retching. Firetrucks screeched up Broadway. She lay listening to the noises, then decided to take a bath. She was about to get into the steaming tub when someone knocked quietly on the door. "It's Molly," a voice said softly. Gina put on her bathrobe and answered the door. "I just came to say hello. Alex called Kevin and we were wondering how you were. This is my friend Vicki." Molly pointed to a tall, willowy girl. "Vicki is the one with every-thing," she went on plaintively. "I've known her since I was three. She cut her teeth first, she got her period first, she grew boobs and I didn't."

Vicki, who was tall and lovely, grinned. "You left out the

best parts. How do you like it here?" she asked Gina, sitting on the table.

"The room service stinks," Molly answered. "The maid refused to clean my room because she said it was too dirty."

"I asked *her*, Molly," Vicki said.

"It's OK. I've only been here a few hours. Do you live here too?"

"No," Vicki said, "I live in the dorms."

"Yeah. The clincher is, Vicki has money. Her father owns a diaphragm factory.

"A diaphragm factory?" Gina repeated, smiling.

"Need a free sample?" Molly asked jokingly. "You and . . . ," she waved her hand.

"It's time for a change," Gina said, trying to sound sophisticated. "Do you know a doctor?" she asked Vicki. She dreaded clinics and questions.

"Go to mine. He's wonderful. A real dream. Don't tell him I sent you for the diaphragm. I went to someone else for mine because he's a friend of my father. Tell him Eddie Lanik—he's my dad—sent you." She took a pen out of her handbag and wrote a name and telephone number on an old envelope. "I wish I could have gone to him."

"If you really want to look out for yourself, take the pill. That's what I do," said Molly. "You really better watch out. Alex is a prince and all; I know he's supposed to be the smartest of all of us and the most elegant," she recited as if intoning a litany she had heard too many times, "but if you ask me he's a self-centered bastard, and his ego is getting bigger by the minute. He's going around telling everybody that you left your crazy Sicilian father just to screw him."

"Molly," Vicki said, "do you always have to shoot your mouth off?"

"It's just what I feel."

"It's OK," Gina said. "It was nice of you both to come," she added, getting up.

"Look," Vicki said, "if you want him, you have him. He's very involved with you. He's bragging about it—so what."

"All I'm saying," Molly broke in, "is that he comes on like he's out of this world, and he's really no different than any of them."

Gina opened the door. "Look, I'm really glad you came. It's just that I'm really tired. I haven't been able to sleep for weeks because of my parents. And I just want to sleep now."

When they had gone she sat down and tried to lift the weight that had fallen on her. It was too late for a bath. The water had cooled and she was too upset to be soothed that easily. Suppose the whole thing was just an ego trip for him. It doesn't matter, she thought, I'm still better off here than there. The phone in the hallway was ringing. Someone thudded toward it. Nobody in this place sleeps, she thought irritably.

"Geenah!" someone screamed. The call was for her. She straightened her bathrobe and went out to the phone.

"Is everything all right?" Alex asked anxiously. "I've been worried about you."

"I was just worrying about me too," she said. "You see how much we have in common."

"Did anyone come?"

"Just Molly and a friend of hers."

"Stay away from them."

"Look, my family isn't going to come tonight. It's too late. What time is it, anyway? If my parents were going to come, they would have." Let him worry, she thought. She wouldn't tell him they didn't know where she was.

There was silence at the other end. "Well," he said finally, "I'll see you tomorrow."

"Yeah. Tomorrow," she said, hanging up the phone. If he's so pleased that I would risk being beaten to a pulp for him, she thought, he should come to stop it from happening. She couldn't get away from the real blast Molly had given to her elation. Her freedom was barely a night old, and already it was dribbling away into nothing. Nobody leaves you alone when you're alone, she thought. She pulled the plug on the now cold bathwater, watching it swirl down the drain.

Vicki's doctor had an office on Park Avenue and Seventy-eighth Street. It had a beautiful marble foyer filled with palms. Three women sat in his waiting room. One was pregnant, but elegantly and beautifully dressed in a sheer linen dress fitted tight at the bodice and falling in graceful gathers from an Empire waist. Gina stared at her wistfully. She had spent real money on a dress she could only wear for a few months. That somehow summed up all the differences between this woman and the ones in her old neighborhood, who had made do with one pair of polyester slacks, a smock top, and skirts widened by an ever-lengthening chain of safety pins. The pins could then be saved for fastening diapers.

Dr. Skogee had been almost too obliging on the telephone. Once she had given Eddie Lanik's name, he said he would fit her in. He really was busy, too. She felt uncomfortable. It was one thing to go to bed with Alex, but something else to admit it. Publicly. A nurse took her aside and asked her some questions, filling out a card. Reason for coming? A checkup and advice about birth control, she said flatly. The nurse took her into an examination room and handed her a bathrobe. Gina undressed and wrapped it around her. It was chilly. It must be thirty degrees in here, she thought. She looked around for a magazine, but there was nothing but medical equipment in the room. After twenty minutes or so, she sat down on the table; after ten more, she curled up on it and closed her eyes.

When the doctor came in, he patted her rump. "Well, how is Eddie?" he said, shaking his head. "I haven't seen him around."

"Neither have I," she answered. Somehow it didn't seem right to tell him she had never met him.

"You know him long?" he asked, washing his hands.

"Not really," she answered.

"But well," he smiled.

She smiled.

The nurse came in and placed some instruments on a tray. She stood next to the table, placing Gina's feet in the stirrups.

"I've never had this kind of examination before," Gina said, covering her eyes.

"Nothing to it," Dr. Skogee said.

"I don't think there's anything wrong with me," she said as he inserted a speculum. "I just want a diaphragm." She felt a slight sting. The idea of a conversation in this position was awful.

"That cervix looks clean as a whistle," he said with conviction. He drew out the speculum. It's over, she thought. But it wasn't. Finally he stood up. "Everything's fine," he said. "The ovaries are maybe a little tender. How many times a week do you have intercourse?" he asked.

"It varies."

"Well, if it's often you might be better off with the pill. Especially if you're not the type of person who remembers. Eddie, though, naturally always advocates the diaphragm." He began to fit her. He was very quick, even quicker explaining how she could check to see if it was in place. When he finished he stood next to the table. "Have a good time," he said, touching her cheek lightly. "And give my best to Eddie."

"Thank you," she answered, not knowing what else to say. "I will."

He shook his head and left.

She stopped at the nurse's desk on the way out. "I would rather pay my bill now," she said, "instead of having it sent."

"The doctor said there would be no charge for the examination or the fitting," the nurse answered, handing her a prescription for a diaphragm.

"That's very kind of him," Gina said, feeling pretty guilty.

"Take care of yourself, dear," the nurse said, dismissing her.

She walked into the September sunlight feeling disturbingly elated. It wasn't right to have let him think she knew Eddie. He thinks I more than know him, she suddenly realized. I even helped him think that. But the slight shame paled before the sense of how easily it had all been done. She had the prescription filled at a drugstore nearby. The pharmacist, standing behind a high glass display case, his face hidden, didn't even bother to look at her. The thought became huge: I can hardly wait to try it out.

She walked through the park and took a bus up Broadway to the Bristol. She bathed. She tried on four different combinations of blouses and skirts before she settled on a white dress. As she went to meet Alex she could see from a distance that he was in a good mood. He was pacing back and forth, looking in all directions. As soon as he spotted her he smiled and waved.

"We're free," he said, "we're free. We can have a whole night."

Why this now, she wondered. What had changed since last night? Maybe he just got used to the idea.

"I have it all planned. We're going to spend a real evening instead of just going to bed together. We're going to a movie!"

"A movie? What movie?" she asked. What movie is better than going to bed with me, she thought.

"This movie is my father's favorite movie," he said, turning her toward downtown. He hugged her to him as they walked. "He took me to see it when I was five. I still remember the first time I saw it. The crowd scene scared me half to death."

"Five is pretty young for crowd scenes. He should have waited until you were six. Six is the right age."

"The first time I saw *Children of Paradise*," he went on, ignoring her, "I was too young to know what it was about. But he wanted me to see it because it was his favorite. I've seen it maybe twelve times and I never get tired of it."

"You like the same things, you and your father?" she asked. Suddenly, he was full of his father. In all the weeks they had been together, he had scarcely mentioned him. Now, all of a sudden, there he was. Nino goes, *his* father appears, when all the while, freedom was there in her bag. She kept thinking about it. She didn't even know if it was because she was excited, or something. She just wanted to see what it was like. Maybe if she told him about it, she thought, he might be curious too.

But he was still talking about his father. "Remarkable," he was saying. "He's the most remarkable person in the world. You're going to meet him. We'll go down to Philadelphia for a weekend. We can do it now. We can borrow his car for a day and drive to the countryside. The hills are fantastic."

"Let's do it," she said insincerely. Somehow, she was lying a lot since she had left home. It already seemed a thousand years ago, even though it was only one night and seven hours. Before, she rarely lied, although she often said nothing. Then she lied about Alex and lied a lot more about where she was when she was really with Alex. Now she was lying to Alex. There's a lesson in this, she thought, but what was it?

When they got to his apartment, he began to rummage through the refrigerator for dinner. He always had a supply of Polish ham, fresh sweet butter, and rye bread. "Next time," he said, putting it all on the table, "why don't you make dinner? Do you cook, and things like that?"

"Sure," she said. "I can do anything. . . ." She giggled.

"Pretty happy with life," he said, grabbing her. "Really high this time," he said, amused.

"Getting better all the time," she agreed. "Why don't you finish dinner for tonight?" She disappeared into the bathroom with her handbag.

After supper they stretched out on his bed and he began nibbling her. "You look like such a a little virgin in white," he said, tickling her. "Why do you wear dresses like that?" He began unbuttoning the top.

"I forget," she said.

"You're my virgin," he said. "Say that."

"Say what?"

"Say you're my virgin."

She murmured something and kissed him. He was running his hands down her back, over her hips, down her thighs. He began nibbling her belly, his teeth moving over her in small striking bites. His tongue moved lower. It flicked inside her. He stiffened, his whole body grew tight. He sat up and spat. "What are you doing with that Ramses junk on?" he demanded.

How does he know it's Ramses? she thought. "What's the matter?" she asked him.

He stuck his fingers inside her and hooked one into the diaphragm. "This is the matter."

It really did look offensive, hanging there on his finger. It had looked so friendly before, on hers.

He walked it like a dog, to the garbage can, stood looking

at it, and then dropped it in. "Go take a bath," he said, "and get that stuff out of you."

"You haven't got a bathtub," she said, wounded. "What's wrong with it? What would we do if I got pregnant?"

"How do you know what I want to do? You never ask me. If you were even thinking of this, you should have mentioned it to me first. You must have known I wouldn't like it," he said angrily, "or you would have told me first."

"There wasn't time to tell you. It just occurred to me last night."

"Where did you find out about these things, anyway? How did you get it? You couldn't have figured this out yourself. You wouldn't have known how."

"Thanks," she said. "It's none of your business." It wasn't much of an answer, but it was a confusing argument. Either way she was losing. If she'd figured it out herself, she lost innocence credit. If she hadn't, she was just someone else's dupe.

"It must have been Molly. I bet I know what she said." He began to mimic her. " 'You have to be your own best friend. Take care of yourself.' "

He was getting to her. "What's the point of making a scene about it? If I'm taking care of myself, I'm taking care of you. You don't want the responsibility of a child any more than I do."

"You're right," he said. "I don't. But this isn't about a child. It's about trust." He was pacing around the room, furious.

Gina began getting dressed.

He watched her. "Talking about this turns me off," he said. "Let's just read or something." He picked up a book. He was not going to notice that she was leaving. She buckled on her sandals. Contraception hasn't improved my sex life, she thought. She stood fully dressed, but indecisive. If she left now, she would really be changing a lot. Exactly what, she didn't know, but she knew it would be a lot.

"Look," she said. "I'm sorry the whole thing happened. I hate arguments. I've been watching them all my life and I'm not going to have any with you. So I think it might be better for me to go home. We can see each other when all this passes," she said.

"If you leave now, it's never going to pass," he said. But when he looked up, she saw his eyes were bright with water. She watched surprised, wondering if the wetness would really become tears. It came to her that she didn't really understand him. This had some meaning for him she couldn't figure out. But before she could make up her mind to go, he came to the door and hugged her.

"Don't leave," he whispered. "Don't leave me now."

If I stay now, it'll mean he's won, she thought. But what was more disturbing was the sudden sense of what she was in for with him. He had seemed never to be at odds with anything. And now in the last couple of days there had been so many moments when he drew lines, reached points he couldn't get beyond. Now he was becoming as gentle as he had been harsh, stroking her neck and back as he unbuttoned her dress. His hands were sweeping the energy, the flight, from her thighs. There are no good choices, she realized, the recognition cutting into the thoughtless pleasure she had taken in the feel of him. Either she went along without the diaphragm, or . . . the alternatives didn't show up. Her thoughts broke down under the pressure of his body, the lovemaking that was somehow more urgent, more desperate than before. He seemed to be everywhere at once, bringing her to the edge of orgasm and stopping, teasing her, running his nails across her back and hips, slipping, wrenching her away from orgasm.

He was hypnotic. He was, she realized dreamily, taking her

over completely; she could feel herself ebbing away. Now he forced her shoulders back against the bed, pinning one with his body and the other with his hand on her arm. He began to lick her face and body. His grip on her shifted and tightened.

"You have to say it now," he murmured. "You have to say you'll do what I want."

"What do you want?" she said, half repeating his question.

"Whatever I want," he said, pressing his lips against her softly.

"Whatever you want," she agreed. "Whatever you want," she repeated, not caring so long as he came back into position.

He pulled her toward him. Orgasm was something to agree on.

Afterward he lay curled against her, dozing off. She had never known such intense emotion. Pleasure had washed through her, peaking and peaking again. She ran her fingers lightly on his face, looking at him as though she had never seen him before. "My God," she murmured. "My God."

It wasn't until the morning that she saw her back was etched with welts and her buttocks were splashed with black-purple bruises. His teeth had cut into the soft even skin of her belly.

It was difficult to believe he had done it. He wasn't tough—compared to Nino he was a marshmallow—but all the same, he was far more dangerous in an unfathomable way. How had it happened? The fight over the diaphragm had made her want to leave. But then he had seemed so stricken, so lost; she had stayed, giving to his vulnerability what she would not give to his anger. Once she had, she had become far more vulnerable to him than he had been to her. She stared at the welts on her back, twisting toward the mirror to see that they began at her shoulders and moved all the way down her back. He had turned the tables on her in a big way. How could she not have felt it? The worst part was that she had found his intensity dazzling. She had lost herself in it, and with that, lost the burden of wariness. Yet look what happened without it, she thought, stunned by the sight of her back.

"I'm sorry," he said, watching her. "I didn't realize . . ." his voice trailed as he saw her finger the blotchy tooth-tattoo.

"It's OK," she said without conviction. Not even the silky light dress lay comfortably on her back. The smoothest fabric would feel like barbed wire for days.

"I just got carried away, I guess," Alex went on.

No you didn't, she thought. You knew exactly what you were doing. The lines of welts ran down her left and right sides, perfectly parallel.

"I never meant to hurt you," he said sheepishly.

"It's really OK," she insisted. "It was worth it," she said, deciding to brazen it out. But they had trouble looking each other in the eye.

"I'll make it up to you," he continued. "I know just the treatment for boo-boos." He put his arms around her.

"I'll bet you do," she answered, forcing a smile. At least he hadn't offered to bathe and dress the cuts. She hated people who hurt you and then offered to repair the damage. "Quack cures are my favorite," she said.

But after he left for work she was not amused. She sat over a cup of tea until it got cold. Then she made another cup and stared into it. He has a tremendous will, she thought. Her desire gave him power over her and he didn't and wouldn't hesitate to use it. It had never occurred to her that he had that kind of will. Where had he kept it all this time? But then, it hadn't occurred to her that she too had a tremendous will, and that she could lose it in the long, clean lines of his body, the hard, muscular stomach, the powerful thighs, the chest flecked with burnished gold hair. Somehow she couldn't say she had lost or he had won. The whole thing was getting into a dimension that was way beyond her. She feared the words there were for these things. Her mind kept moving from desire to self-doubt to fear of where that road could lead. But by the time the second cup of tea had cooled, she brought herself back to questions she could answer.

Clearly, she had botched the whole business of the diaphragm. She couldn't bring it up again; he was too intolerant. No, it wasn't just that. He couldn't take the barrier she set up, even though, in his way, he was full of walls himself. What had turned him on, she could see, was her being susceptible, vulnerable, unprotected. The issue is, she said to herself, are you going to go on using nothing, as he wants, or not. What would be the right thing to do?

She liked problems that could be reduced to choices because everything else was becoming a mystery. Alex was manipulative and deep. You could not know where you stood with him because you could not predict what he would do or when he would shift his stance. He didn't care for physical force or intimidation; that had made her think he was tender. But he had won through begging her not to go what could not be extracted in other ways. Disarm and advance, she thought sourly. It worked. It was subtle, seductive, masked with embraces, an antagonism you would have to locate among jokes and caresses. One thing was for sure, she thought, it would never pay to cross him directly. Whenever she did, he would shift ground and outmaneuver her. If she insisted on using something, she would outrage him. If she went along with him, sooner or later she would get pregnant.

There seemed to be only one way to go. That was to appear to yield to him completely, to keep the surface of their time together perfect. He would hate her if she spoiled it or confronted him, she knew, shrugging uncomfortably in the dress that barely touched her sensitive skin. She wasn't ready to give him up. But she wouldn't let him spoil it for her either. She rummaged in her bag for her address book.

When she reached Dr. Skogee, she tried for a voice more self-assured than any she had used before.

"One of my friends," she said, trying to sound worldly, "objects to the diaphragm. What do you think of the rhythm system?"

"I think you better find another friend," Dr. Skogee said, amused. He called for her chart and hesitated for a minute. "You'd be better off on the pill. I'll write you a prescription. Stop in at my office this afternoon and pick it up. If I can, I'll come out to explain how to use it. If not, I'll leave instructions with Mrs. Johnson."

"Thanks," she said gratefully. "You've been really wonderful."

"Not at all," he said politely. "Keep in touch. I'd like to talk to you sometime."

"I'll look forward to that." She hung up.

But when she got to his office, he had already left for the hospital. Mrs. Johnson gave her instructions and a prescription. She filled the prescription at the same drugstore she had gone to before, and slipped the round plastic disc into a zippered compartment in her bag.

Some problems were easy to solve. Once you could reduce trouble to the issue of choices, the mystery, the insolubility of things was put into place. It hit her that Nino might have become rigid because he couldn't deal with anything ill-defined either. He was contemptuous of what he called "confusion." But life was lived in what he would call confusion. Anyway, what a friend Dr. Skogee had turned out to be. And she would never have gotten to him without Vicki. Gratitude poured out of her into the bright afternoon. The raw sensitivity of her skin seemed to subside in the fullness of how well it all seemed to work out. Alex would get what he wanted; she would get what she wanted. No one had to know. That meant, she suddenly realized, that she would be lying to him all the time, especially in bed. For a moment that shadowed her good feeling. You shouldn't lie to someone you love. Especially when they're giving you so much pleasure. But then, she thought, you shouldn't work someone over you love, either. It was hard to tell which was more wrong, her lying or his bruising her.

Sooner or later, Gina realized, she would have to be more direct with Alex. When he put together what she did and what she seemed to be doing, it might not work out anymore. Maybe it shouldn't. Would she have gone this far if it hadn't been for Nino, Nino the know-it-all, setting her up for what he wanted least? It had worked out that way. There was a limit to how many moves she could make, one after the other. And anyway, the freedom she had won had to have something else in it to mean anything. There had to be some purpose that had nothing to do with anyone but her.

In a way, she thought, the pills served the purpose, but they could never be it. The purpose itself had more to do with the elation of waking up in the morning alone in her room, with the pale morning light enlivening the tiny plant that grew between the bathroom tiles, and that she watered drop by drop. It had to do with the sense of joy that she was alive, that the day had not even begun, but was all ahead to be lived fully, or to be wasted, as she wished. There was a voluptuous density in the feel of the sun on her body, in the sweet shock of diving into the gym pool at Hunter, of cutting the water, lap after lap, of simply moving, moving, moving.

So what did it matter, really, if Alex had depths she hadn't fathomed, so long as she could cut through them for now. What counted was that it all worked out. She fingered the disc and took it out. Each pill, precisely in its pocket, no ungainly pile in a bottle, but a neat, efficient clockwork that reset biological time, that said, Take it day by day. Her mind was turning toward the one all-absorbing issue: when she would try it out. This time is wasn't a question of his desire. It was a matter of her body chemistry. Which, she thought, losing herself in the memory of the night before, was showing odd tendencies.

She makes me feel clumsy, thought Alex, bringing the arm of his papercutter down on a sheet of stamps. She does it by never saying what she thinks. Speech pours out of her, but she never gives anything away.

He shoved in another sheet of stamps.

There were a lot of silences in a day with her. Her silences were always what they call "pregnant," but if you expected information, all you got—he crunched down the arm, angrily—was an abortion. I've done enough work for these people today, he thought irritably. Usually he worked on a ratio of one to three: one hour for them and three for himself, to preserve his sanity. To be fair, he thought, one hour of his was as good as five of anybody else's, so they came out ahead anyway. He picked up a briefcase full of folders. There was a story he had begun for her. On the first page was a drawing with the caption "Princess Persephone." It softened him. Maybe he was just building a case against her. He often got mad at women when he felt he had done something bad to them, whatever it was. It was, he thought, looking through the first page, a pretty fable.

"Once upon a time, many years ago, near the forests where the lions live, dwelled the strangest beast on earth. It was stronger than a lion and perfectly black. . . . " No, he thought, maybe some other day. It was to be for her birthday, but that was still a few months away. And he didn't feel like giving her presents now.

He opened another folder. This one said "Maid Marian." That's it, he thought, beginning to read over what he had written:

It is impossible to believe that Fabio was born: that he and his twin sister Lulu had twisted and narrowed in the birth canal of a bumpkin Chicago woman. For if his sister had become a true daughter of the South Side, Fabio was more a princeling than an ordinary boy, and grew into a man of extraordinary beauty. His face was as elegant as any courtier's, his eyes fine as the most skillful of falconers. But it is difficult to know what Fabio saw, for he saw so strangely. And often he spoke words that were palpable—strange shapes unfamiliar as the pollen of the rarest flowers. Yet somehow they were recognizable, as fragments of dreams are. For what man in his sleeping or waking hours has not envisaged shapes in his soul that never appear on earth? And perhaps that is what beauty is: something secretly shining.

Alex took the page out of the folder, crumpled it, and threw it in the wastebasket. He could feel the pressure of being alone with her tonight. It wasn't what he wanted. Maybe it was time to take her to Philadelphia. A little trip, a little distance—it would be just right.

"The bus," he told Gina that night, "leaves at eight tomorrow morning. So pack tonight. In fact, I'll help you." His mother was so critical of how everyone looked. And it was getting cool enough to need to wear real clothes. He went to her dresser and rummaged through. He took out some blouses, selected what he wanted, and put back the rest. Then he looked in the closet for a moment. She had nice things. She had the clothes of a girl with money. You had to find out for yourself that her mother had made all of them from remnants. He picked out a burgundy mohair skirt and folded it into the bag. "You can wear this in the morning," he said, pointing to a dress, olive green, with a narrow waist and full skirt. "All set," he said.

"All set," she repeated. It was all there; all she had to do was smile, and what would be the point of doing otherwise? What would be the point of preferring the blouses he had left in the drawer to the ones he had put in the bag? His eyes were soft; he seemed particularly vulnerable. Maybe he was afraid his parents wouldn't like her. So was she—she wasn't doing well with parents lately. But it seemed better not to say anything, and certainly not to ask whether he thought his parents would be difficult. By now she knew he hated complications; he just couldn't deal with them. Mama used to say—the words ran through her mind—"Never tell a man your troubles, because you can be sure he doesn't want to hear them anyway."

Alex could walk through anybody's mudfield and come out shining like a prince. And that was how he looked, even in the Port Authority Bus Terminal at eight the next morning, carrying her bag. Only half awake, she could see that the terminal's bedraggled, exhausted inmates—the junkies, prostitutes, and crazies—seemed plugged into a universal hangover. Alex, in white corduroy, wide awake, chattered happily, oblivious to everything else. On the bus, he curled up, put his head on her lap, and fell asleep. She watched him for a while, stroking the soft white skin set off by his beard. Sometimes it shocked her to realize how little they really knew about each other. All my life, she thought, I've lived right up against other people, but I've never felt really close to any of them. Intimacy—in-ti-ma-cy—the word was still a mystery. It was a physical thing, she thought clumsily, the sensation of flowing into each other. That way she came to feel connected to him.

The thought of the days and evenings they had made love in his white, lit room, watching the sun make shadows on the white blinds, rushed through her. She touched his hair lightly, so as not to wake him. The trouble was, the words they spoke didn't flow into each other in the same way. It upset him to hear what he didn't want to hear. So she had stopped telling him. She was grateful for the Bristol. She didn't have to live with him, and somehow, she thought, that was preserving their intimacy, the delicious, almost dangerous closeness they sometimes did achieve. Too much proximity, she thought, maybe that would just ruin the intimacy. She was feeling silly. What would she say to his parents? She would have to talk, but what was there to talk about? I'll do my best, she thought resignedly. All you can do is your best. There it went again. She shook her head.

Why did she always have to be thinking in words Nino and Laura always used? In the relief of being away from them— were they as glad, she wondered, to be rid of her?—she hadn't missed them at all. They had clearly decided to ignore her. She had scarcely even thought of them. It was probably wrong to have blotted them out so easily. She knew she was supposed to feel dread, guilt, or something. But she didn't. There was too much else happening. She looked at Alex sleeping in her lap. He was so beautiful. If only he weren't quite so—brittle.

Even in sleep Alex looked wry. He had an air of amusement much of the time, as though the actions of others entertained him without involving him. Was Victor—his father—like that too? He had to be different. Victor had arrived. He was a real success. His five-volume history of the Puritan settlements and the Indian wars was a classic. She had read part of it for an American history course and could see why it had won prizes. His books on the American Revolution and the Constitution were supposed to be even better. You couldn't do work like that without a commitment that lasted for years. In addition to being a scholar, he had served in France and the Netherlands for the State Department and the United States Information Service. He had made it on talent and drive, a fitting achievement for a Puritan scholar who believed in the work ethic. The religion of effort and rectitude. Alex was not a believer.

They must make an odd pair, Victor and Alex, Gina thought. Alex had no tolerance for anything that didn't amuse him. He had no regard for disciplined effort. It was part of his charm, but it was also very annoying. Last week she was studying for a French exam and he wanted to go out. He grabbed the book and made jokes about how ridiculously useless everything in it was. He was probably right. He had grown up speaking French during the years his father had worked in Paris. But what did that matter if you knew no French at all and studying was a way to begin. When she pointed that out, he had dismissed her with "Well, you'll get an *A* anyway!" That wasn't the point either. She liked the confidence that came from being certain of what you knew, even if it meant going over things more than was strictly necessary. Alex had his own sense of priorities, but he liked throwing hers out of kilter. He was shrewd about it, too. He did it through ridicule, making fun of the books she was reading. Through. . . . The chain of thought was beginning to bring her down. It was full of rancor. You're beginning to dislike him, she thought, gazing at him. Still, she was curious about his parents. Maybe they held a clue to what he was.

By the time they reached the house, her mouth was filled with speeches of thanks for the invitation. But no one was there. The idea that parents could invite you for the weekend—their own son!—and be too busy to be home when he arrived was so alien, she took it personally. It must be a message to her.

A note on the foyer table said they were out for the day; lunch was in the refrigerator, and they would be back at five.

"How disappointing," she said.

"Not at all," he answered. "We'll have time to get settled." They walked through the house. It was large, rambling, a huge colonial filled with little extra rooms and balconies.

"It's really lovely," Gina said admiringly. "Your mother has wonderful things." There were sheer fishnet curtains, blues and mauves, thrown together casually with a startling effect.

"Yes," Alex said. "She does. She came from a very wealthy family. She and my father have never had much money, but she's always known how to make wherever we were look like this," he said, waving his arm.

"Where is she from?" Gina asked.

"She's from Boston originally."

"And your father?" she asked, forgetting he had already told her.

"Ohio."

"How did they meet?"

Alex shrugged. She trailed him through the house.

"This will be your room."

"We'll have separate rooms here?" she asked. She had expected that.

"Yes, I think it's best."

"Well," she said, stretching out on the bed, "it's good to lie down. I wasn't ready to get up before seven." She patted a place on the bed next to her.

"No," he said.

"No one will be here before five," she said.

"I just don't want to. Let's go out for a walk."

"We just came in."

"We'll go to the museum."

"Is it nearby?" she asked.

"No, of course not. We can take a bus."

"We just got off a bus," Gina objected.

"Why are you being so difficult?" he snapped.

"I'm not. I just want to rest for a minute. I'd like to see the museum. Just give me a minute. Could I make some tea?" she asked.

"I'll do it," he said. "You'd better unpack your things or they'll be wrinkled."

He seemed so tense she thought he was just upset about how she would look to his parents. She hung everything up, disappointed by his grimness.

In front of the Matisses she grew more relaxed, letting the colors wash through her. Alex became more tense as the afternoon wore on, scarcely speaking to her. By the time they got back it was six, and the house was filled with people. A handsome woman in her middle-fifties came to the door when they entered. Her heavy blond hair was streaked with gray and rolled smoothly back from her face into a neat twist.

"Here you are at last," she said lightly. "We wondered what had happened to you. Why didn't you leave a note?" she demanded of Alex, ignoring Gina.

"We've been at the museum," Alex answered, motioning to Gina. "This is my mother, Catherine."

"I'm happy to meet you," Gina said awkwardly.

"Of course," Catherine said, still ignoring Gina. "We invited a few friends we thought you'd like to see. Maxine and Jordan and some new people. Come in," she said, finally gesturing to Gina too.

"Excuse me," Gina said. "I'd like to wash and change, if it's all right."

"There's a small bathroom off your bedroom, to the right," Catherine said. "No one will bother you there."

"Thank you," Gina said.

She slipped away to her room and laid out the mohair skirt and a print blouse and went in to wash her arms and face. There was talc and scented soap in the bath. More than the comforts of home. It would have been great to run a hot bubble bath, but there wasn't time. If she did, Alex would think she was trying to avoid the whole thing. And he would be right. So she put on stockings and shoes with high heels, the skirt and blouse, and brushed her hair. A blusher and some lipstick. That's it, she thought. That's the way I look.

When she was leaving her room, she met Alex at the door.

"I was coming for you," he said. "Come and meet everyone." He seemed very happy.

At the entrance to the living room Alex paused. An older woman at the other end of the room called his name and everyone turned and looked at them.

"Hello," he said. "This is my . . . "—he made a great show of looking helplessly for a word—"friend, Gina."

Everyone laughed. Gina felt stung, embarrassed. Why did he have to make such a point of it? She could see Catherine hadn't liked that at all. Alex's mother came toward her with an older woman. Her eyes had turned even cooler. They raked her over, lingered on her face and hair, took in her clothes, recoiled from her shoes, and found the whole, Gina could see, unacceptable.

The other woman had a ready smile. She reached for Gina's hand and said to Alex, "So this is what you've been doing, the reason you're too busy to come crosstown to visit me," she said. "I have known Alex since he was seven," she said. "I would do anything for him except make him eat spinach. And I have to wait until we both come to Philadelphia to see him when I live ten minutes away in New York."

Gina laughed, liking her. "So you don't live down here," she said.

"Never. The weather in New York is bad enough. You come to see me and make him come along," she said, turning away. Alex's mother had moved on to another guest.

"That's my father," Alex said, nodding toward a tall man across the room.

Looking at Victor from a distance, Gina saw little of Alex in him. Spare and angular, he stood smiling and polished in a dark blue suit and striped silk tie. He looked as though he had found the way to an endless prime. Alex had joked about his father's fitness craze, his daily two-mile run, his determined efforts to learn squash, his victory over his love of sausages and beer. It had paid off. Alex had reminded her of a slide she had seen in art history of Donatello's sculpture of David. David is all physical grace. He's wearing a fantastic hat, and leaning on his sword as one foot lightly rests on the severed head of Goliath. He's just killed the giant, but he seems not to have fought him, to have done him in effortlessly. The delicacy of David seemed to reflect Alex's code: no sweat. Victor was rugged by comparison.

Gina could see Victor moving through the cocktail party talking to everyone. He was deft. His face was not expressive, a social mask, correct and diplomatic, a face for making inquiries but giving no answers. Several times his eyes had met hers and he had smiled. When Alex had introduced her—flourishing his pregnant pause—as his "friend," Victor had not been pleased. He had looked from her to Alex to see how she had taken it and whether Alex had gotten what he wanted out of it. She had felt embarrassed, but decided to deal with it the way Alex dealt with everything. She looked amused. Victor's subsequent glances toward her showed she had done well.

This one is younger than the others, Victor thought, and more dramatic in style. Her clothes are more of a costume than an outfit—carefully chosen for effect. Her bold colors stand out in a room in which women wear black dresses and interesting pieces of jewelry. Her hair is swept up and coiled in a braid instead of a chignon. The effect is striking rather than stylish.

Victor began to make his way across the room to her when a tall blonde—she must be almost six feet tall, Gina thought—took Victor's arm. He propelled her toward Gina while the woman kept talking animatedly to him.

"She's inviting me to lunch in New York," Victor said. "What do you think of that?"

"You're the most interesting person to have lunch with. Anyway, I promise to let you come back here, sooner or later." The woman laughed.

"What do you think of that?" Victor repeated.

"I think she has excellent taste," Gina said, not really sure what was going on between them.

"Oh, well, she's right," the woman announced to Victor. "Out of the mouths of babes," she said, pulling Victor toward the bar. He permitted himself to be pulled.

Pretty smooth, Victor thought. And the daughter of the inarticulate woman who had spoken to him from Alex's apartment. Alex had said almost nothing about her; just that she was making him happy—he really thought people existed for that!—and that she came from a strict Italian family that wanted him to marry her. He had called her father a real "primitive." She didn't look primitive. On the contrary, she seemed to have no visible rough edges. She carried herself beautifully. Her body seemed perfectly balanced and her movements had a freedom and strength that contrasted with her air of reserve and containment. Alex had told him she was studying anthropology in college, but he was vague about everything else.

When the last guest had left, Gina picked up a plate to help Catherine collect the leftovers.

"These are wonderful," she said to Catherine. "How do you make them?"

"I didn't. I buy everything and have it delivered," Catherine replied, taking the plate from her and putting it back down on the table. "Let's sit down for a while until Elaine is through in the kitchen. She'll be in to clean up. He can help her," Catherine said, gesturing toward the bartender. "Is anyone hungry for dinner?"

Victor shrugged. "I am always ready for dinner. I never eat these things." He waved his hand over the hors d'oeuvres.

"I made a feast of them, as usual," Alex said.

"I'm not hungry," Gina added.

Catherine sighed. Victor always expected dinner. She went into the kitchen to tell Elaine to set the table and took a casserole out of the freezer. She set the microwave herself. She always had Elaine make a few of these casseroles for the freezer. That way dinner was always ready. Although by the time it was over, Elaine would have gone home and she would have to clean up.

She couldn't get a fix on Gina. She was very correct. There wasn't a thing to object to about her, and somehow that was objectionable. She was very good-looking. Her blouse was cut high, to the neck. Nothing was exposed. But she moved very well and her body seemed to radiate an electricity. She reminded Catherine of a lioness wearing a costume. The image made her smile.

Why should she be so suspicious of the girl? She wasn't the first Alex had brought here and she probably wouldn't be the last. If she were on the prowl, Alex was a strange choice of game to hunt. It tore her heart to see him. She could barely look at the elegance of his face or listen to him talk without a stab of pain that nothing was coming of his first-rate looks and his first-rate mind. Her friends had sons who were economists or lawyers or *something* by now. And hers was a part-time clerk and a part-time student of God knows what.

It was embarrassing; worse, it was frightening. How long could he go on like this? If Gina thought she was in for an easy ride, she was in for a fall. Victor kept telling Catherine she thought nobody was good enough for Alex. But the trouble was that Alex wasn't good enough for Alex, either. He had a future, but no present that led up to it. His future was beginning to look like a mirage. He was already twenty-six and still without anything that meant anything to him. Catherine returned to the living room in time to see that Victor had paid the bartender. He settled himself back on the sofa with a tall drink he insisted was his last. She sat near Alex.

Gina surveyed the trio. Catherine had taken off her shoes and put her feet on an ottoman in front of an easy chair that seemed twice her size. Victor sat at one end of a deep sofa with Alex at the other. Gina sat facing them, wondering about them all. An unusual family. There were advantages to being female here. One of them was that there would be no Nino to grill you about your intentions. In this group, she thought wryly, there would certainly be no questions about baseball trivia. Still, she could see they were curious about her, with an inquisitiveness they had not yet shaped into questions.

When in doubt, seize the initiative, she thought. When in fear, seize it faster. She was feeling giddy from the wine she had drunk on an empty stomach. She could start with something safe, just to break the silence.

"How did you get interested in the Puritans and the Indian wars?" she asked Victor. He must have been asked that question a thousand times, she realized.

"What boy can resist tales of Indians, war whoops, noble fighting?"

"You mean the Indians were noble warriors. Your Puritans aren't too wonderful."

"What don't you like about them?"

"You described how they promised not to harm the Indians if they surrendered and converted to Christianity. And then they sold them into slavery in the West Indies once they gave up their weapons. Then there was the hypocrisy of calling them savages for scalping, and then scalping *them* and wearing their scalps as trophies. Not a noble thing for Puritans to do."

Victor looked amused. So that's where Alex gets that look, Gina thought. Except Alex has it most of the time.

"The Indians scalped first," Victor said, tongue in cheek.

"But that was the way they had always done things. The Puritans claimed those ways were heathen and then found themselves following them. That's what interests you, isn't it? Their going into the wilderness and being changed by it rather than simply changing it."

"Don't get him started," Alex said, "or he'll talk all night."

"Yes," Catherine agreed. "This is no time for lectures."

"That's it, isn't it?" Gina asked. "To defeat the enemy you have to see through his eyes, become him, think like him. The more you do, the more you lose yourself, your moral bearings." Gina felt oddly agitated, as though she were saying something truer about herself than anyone else.

Alex groaned.

"Let's go into my study," Victor said, "and leave these people to their small talk. I have some old pictures and manuscripts you might like to see." He rose and motioned for her to follow him. They passed down a corridor into a room lined with books and dominated by a huge desk. Files lined the wall in back of the desk.

"There's some truth in what you say," Victor said, offering her a chair. "But becoming the other, the enemy, also gives you a different perspective in a positive way, permitting greater flexibility in coming to terms with reality."

"How can there be flexibility in matters of life and death? It's one or the other."

"There has to be flexibility there most of all. The stakes have to be high to make you want to see the meaning of your actions in terms of good and evil, to feel the sense of mission. Their sense of destiny took over, they were fired with religious fervor. . . ."

"But all of that made them use the notion of doing right to do what they wanted to do anyway. They did what was expedient and called it right."

"And once the Indians were effectively squelched, they achieved nothing but the sense of possibility." Victor opened a cabinet in one of the bookcases and took out a bottle of Chivas Regal. He reached in for two small glasses, filled them, and handed one to Gina.

She realized that she had already had enough to drink, but took it anyway. She had never tasted whiskey straight.

"Possibility," Victor went on. "*I dwell in Possibility, a fairer house than Prose / more numerous of windows, Superior of Doors.* Infinite possibility." He sipped his drink.

"How could the Puritans believe in fate and predestination and also believe in infinite possibility?" Gina asked.

"That was maybe the ultimate triumph of the wilderness," Victor said, "the undoing of the religion. After all, it grew weaker and weaker until it scarcely existed at all. As a religion. And then Emerson concludes: *There should be no such thing as fate.* There you are. No more Puritans, no more predestination, just a belief in the power of individuals to transform themselves."

"There is no such thing as infinite possibility," Gina said. She caught herself before she said anything about being hemmed in by obligations, by family. Emerson was certainly an improvement. "But change is a kind of doom, too. You know the character in Dante's *Inferno* whose punishment is to keep changing from one thing to another. . . ." She realized she was ceasing to make sense.

"Everything's an open question for you, isn't it?" Victor said, amused.

"You're very good to talk about all this. I mean, I know you already took five volumes to say what you thought about it."

"No, no. I don't mind," Victor protested, finishing off his drink. "Nobody has asked me about it for a long time. And what do you do?"

"I'm at Hunter College, studying anthropology."

"So that's why you like Indians. What will you do when you run through primitive tribes? There are no new ones," he teased.

"I'll study historians," Gina retorted.

Victor laughed. "What's so interesting about my tribe?"

"How they reconcile facts and poetry."

Victor smiled. She was fun, and very young. She would mellow with time, but she was lively company now. "Actually, I have something more interesting to talk about. I had an ulterior motive in bringing you in here."

"Oh?" Gina asked, putting down her drink. "What could it be?"

"It could be lots of things, but it's something we have in common."

"What could we have in common?"

"Alex."

"I'm not claiming joint ownership," Gina said.

"Maybe you should."

"Why is that?"

"It would give you more of a stake in what happens between you—in making it work." Victor realized how much he wanted it to work. There was something decent and solid about her. She would be good for Alex.

"Machines work," Gina said. "People are either happy or unhappy together."

"It's not that simple," Victor persisted.

"*You* obviously feel Alex needs working on. What do you want to fix?"

Victor looked at her. "Do you always get to the point as quickly as that?"

"You led the way."

"Do you know what Alex intends to do?"

"About what?"

"About school. Does he want to finish in New York? Is he taking courses that will help him finish? Does he want to go elsewhere?"

"Not that I know of. He's taking a course in Chinese."

Victor winced. "Does he go to class?"

"Why don't you ask him?"

"He doesn't answer my questions."

"I can't be your informer in the enemy camp."

"He's not my enemy," Victor said.

"Then talk to him. I can't be a go-between," Gina said gently. It ran through her mind that Victor must be pretty desperate, or more drunk than he seemed, to talk this way to someone he had never met before. "You're really worried about him, aren't you? You think he's wasting his time."

"I *know* he's wasting his time. He's already wasted years. Not to mention an expensive education. He's got to do something for himself. It won't be easier next year than this one."

"What makes you think I could help?" Gina was getting more depressed by the minute. It was one thing to be irritated now and then by Alex's laxity, but another to hear his own father say it was a catastrophe.

"You're the first woman he's brought here in a long time. He must really care for you. You seem . . . all there. Does that sound funny?"

"You think he's not all there?" Gina smiled.

"I don't know anymore."

"Why do you think he isn't doing more?"

Victor shook his head.

"Maybe you expect too much. He's doing what he wants to be doing. Isn't that enough?"

"He'll never be happy doing nothing, going nowhere, not living up to his potential," Victor said.

"Why do you think he lives the way he does?"

"To get back at me."

"Why should he want to do that?"

"Why does anyone hurt himself to get back at someone else?" Victor looked at her directly. "I know what you're saying when you refuse to get involved. It's what anyone would say. I can't really expect you to say otherwise. All the same, I don't believe you like what he's doing or think it should last. It seems like temporary stuff to you. But he's been doing things like it for six years. Anything that goes on that long isn't temporary. It's a way of life. A rut. If you can do anything to get him out of it, please do it. I haven't succeeded; maybe you won't either. He and I are getting too old to be at each other's throats."

"You don't seem to be angry with each other."

"That's his genius. He knows how to frustrate me while being perfectly pleasant."

Gina looked at him, not knowing what to say. He had spoken with the weary disgust of someone resigned to chronic pain. He's really given up on him, Gina thought. He's written him off as a total failure. He hadn't wanted to, but he had. He was harder and more cutting in his way than Nino. For Nino, if you did the right thing, that was sufficient success.

It was what you were that mattered, not what you became. Here you had to be a star at something to retain your position in the family. Victor was tired of being the father of someone who was still finding himself.

In the silence, kitchen sounds became audible. Gina sat wondering what to say, and was finally saved from having to reply when Alex came to the door.

"You can come in to dinner now," Alex announced. "Everyone else did all the work, and it's time for the defender of the work ethic to come in and freeload." He smiled amiably.

Victor tried to smile back.

Alex looked from Gina to Victor. "Who's been preaching to whom? Any converts here besides me?"

"What have you been converted to?" Gina asked.

"The oldest religion of all. The one with the most followers. At last, I've joined the mob."

"So?" Gina said.

"Cynicism. I don't believe in anything."

"You're lying," Catherine said, coming up behind him. "You believe in dinner. Come in," she insisted, "before everything gets cold."

They followed Catherine into the dining room and settled themselves around the table. Catherine could not shake her resentment of Gina. The last thing Alex needed was a responsibility, a serious involvement with babies and a wife. He wasn't even ready to take care of himself. If he had put himself in a position to have to take care of anyone else, he would never accomplish anything. At least there was hope as long as he was alone. The strain of the party, of smiling at guests and making arrangements, was making her edgy.

"What lovely friends you have," Gina said clumsily to Catherine. "I enjoyed meeting them."

"They are the few good friends who remain with us whatever happens," Catherine answered coolly. She was troubled. Alex had walked away from her before she could ask him what she had wanted to know. And so she asked it now. "Is there any reason," she said delicately, "why you both would be in a rush to do anything drastic?"

"Drastic?" Alex said. "Everything I do is drastic."

"I mean," Catherine continued, "is there any reason why you should rush into marriage?"

Victor looked surprised. Alex said nothing. Gina hated other people's silences.

"What makes you think we're in a rush to do anything?" she asked.

"I just had a sense," Catherine answered.

"If you want to know whether I'm pregnant," Gina said flatly, "the answer is no, I'm not."

It was not the right thing to have said. It hung there in the silence. "But I am tired," she continued. "It's been such a long and full day, I would like to go to sleep." She got up and walked to her room.

"Why did you have to say that?" demanded Alex, following her upstairs.

"It was what she wanted to know; it was what she meant," Gina answered.

"You didn't have to put it so bluntly. You embarrassed her for asking the question to begin with."

"It was an embarrassing question to have asked. She shouldn't have asked it in front of me."

He let that pass. His hands were clenched into fists like tight little balls. "I won't have you making her look like a vulgar inquisitor," he said. "You realize you expose your own vulgarity by pointing, by making an issue of her curiosity."

"It has nothing to do with vulgarity. You can tell from the way she looks at me that she can't stand me," Gina said. She kept talking despite Alex's gestures of protest. "There isn't even anything personal in it. She would probably hate any-body you brought here."

Laura had been right. Alex was strange. She would never know what he thought. She could not have predicted how tense he had been since they had arrived. Still, he was right; her reply to Catherine had been crude. This place, she thought, looking at the tastefully furnished room, is a mine-field. She had walked into it like a fool. Victor thinks a woman could be Alex's salvation. Catherine doesn't. She was trying to provoke me, Gina realized. Maybe she was trying to provoke Victor, too. Victor wants me as a caretaker for Alex; Catherine wants me out of his life. She realized, as she saw the hostility in Alex's eyes, that in his distaste and his mother's, and in Victor's fondness for her, they had divided into factions. It came to her that his parents were probably always working at cross-purposes and shooting down each other's hopes. Now she and Alex were caught in the cross fire. She reached for Alex's hand, ready to apologize for what she had said. But he turned from her and walked out of the room.

Five

Nino's fever was the steadiest thing around. It had come on slowly and settled in. Nothing huge about it, just a persistent heat that broke everything up a little faster. Since the day he had come home to find his right toes darkened to a blackish green, the only thing that seemed to be whole was his gloom. He had soaked his foot in iodine, taken penicillin for days; but the nails and then the flesh of his toes kept darkening, and the pain in his arch and ankles was beginning to move upward. His thirst never stopped now. He drank what seemed like gallons of water every day, but nothing he did washed away the pain.

When you have trouble with something, you keep having trouble with it, he said to himself. I was born crippled and I'll die that way. He couldn't remember his twisted legs or how they had looked. But he remembered his mother carrying him at four and five through clinic after clinic in Palermo, determined to drop his deformity in the lap of someone who could fix it. "It can be taken away," she would tell him over and over. She had finally found a surgeon willing to try. He could almost summon the feel of the long cast that had immobilized him for what seemed like years. "You have to suffer to be well," his mother would say. For years after he came out of the casts able to walk, every time he ran for a ball he seemed to run into the fact that he owed her everything. He had named Gina after her, hoping it would do some good. He had put so much into that child—his hope, his need for someone to talk to. He plunged his foot into a basin of soapy water, wincing at the heat. It was all for nothing. He poured iodine into the water. For nothing. She didn't care for him, for any of them. He lifted his foot out of the basin, watching the brown water drip off onto the white towel. It all added up, all his effort, to this: the flaking, peeling, cracked skin, the progressive darkening he knew, no matter what he said, was gangrene.

One breakdown produces another. She could walk away from him just like that, cracking everything he had kept together with workdays that never ended before midnight, long years of listening to Laura, digging in in front of the ball game just to keep from screaming. Now she won't even call me, he thought. She thinks I'll come and get her again to drag her back. "Let her rot," he said, pouring iodine directly into the cracking toe. At least the burning pain proved it was still alive. He refused to admit he carried around dead parts of himself, hauling them along the streets, hiding them in socks and shoes all stained with useless witches' brew. "Next week," Laura had yelled at him, "you'll start burying potatoes under the drainpipes outside, like my Aunt Concetta did to get rid of her warts!"

If they cut away what's dead, he thought, staring at his leg, there will be nothing left. He wouldn't give in to this. If it was a question of will, he had it. Either you did, or you didn't. He did. The trouble was so did she. His was greater. She had gotten away from it for the moment, but life would get her, even if he hadn't. "Let her rot," he repeated. "We'll rot together."

The fever was making him so weak, there were times he couldn't separate his exhaustion from his anger. He stank of iodine, ammonia, soap. It was one of the neighborhood children who played outside who had made him dose himself sometimes just for the smell.

"You smell like snails," the child had said in his six-year-old's voice.

"What an imagination," Nino had said to him. "Your imagination has a nose!"

Better to stink of iodine than to stink of the grave.

When Laura came in he was sleeping. He had dropped off, lying there, forgetting to put on his socks. She went to the kitchen carrying a huge bag of fruit. After she had washed the apples and peeled him an orange, she went in to see him. When she looked at his foot, she knew it was over. The idiot, she thought. He has diabetes and he thinks he can cure it with iodine and a Band-Aid. And him with a diploma. She was furious. The great thing about fury is that it keeps away everything else. When you aren't angry, then you can think clearly. And if you can think clearly, you can see the future realistically. And her future with him was all there in his black foot, in its prediction that he would soon be legless. The prospect hung there, behind her anger, waiting.

Dr. Rizelli, when she called him, wouldn't come. "You can't afford a house call," he said. "It's thirty-five dollars."

"Come," she said evenly. "I'll pay you in cash."

He was there within the hour to pocket his money and shake his head. "It's hopeless," he said. "I told you that surgery two years ago wouldn't work. What good is eight inches of clear artery when the rest is full of sludge? He should be in the hospital. His diabetes looks out of control. No one can take off that foot unless it's brought under control first. I can do it. I'll arrange for a room."

"No thanks," said Laura. "I'll make my own arrangements."

Dr. Rizelli shrugged.

"Should I wake him up?" Laura asked. "Is there anything you can do for him now?"

"Let him sleep," the doctor said. "What's the point? Good luck." He turned away and left.

He'd need more than luck if he let you put a knife to him, Laura thought. She called Dr. Ginori and waited for him to call back. By midnight there was still no call. Nino woke, freezing in the soaked sheets. Laura changed the sheets and covered him with blankets in which he began to steam. Discussing the symptoms with Laura the next morning, Dr. Ginori told her to bring Nino to the hospital right away. By the time they arrived, Nino was too weak to do more than acknowledge the good fortune Dr. Ginori said he had.

"You got two good years out of that plastic artery I put in," he pointed out, "but the degeneration around it is just too severe. The other leg has no viable arteries to contribute. Neither, as I recall, do your arms. Sometimes," he shrugged, "we just have to accept human limitations. We'll get the diabetes under control, then we have no choice but to remove the gangrened part of the leg." He shook his head. He looked at Nino and met his eyes. "I'm sorry. I wish there were more I could do, but there isn't."

Nino nodded. When Laura wheeled him out, he sank deeper into his chair and closed his eyes. She could see all hope falling apart. He'll never walk again, she thought. His illness closed in on her; what he would have to go through hung there horribly before her. The vision of him, legless, began to fill her mind.

"You can learn to use crutches, or maybe an artificial leg. Jimmy walks everywhere with that artificial leg they gave him when he got out of the army," she said to Nino.

"Jimmy is twenty-two," Nino answered.

"So? You're not so old. How old is sixty? Sixty is nothing these days. You have to try. You're sick now, so you don't think ahead. But you have to. And you have to realize that once the pain is over, you'll want to try to walk."

Nino turned his face toward the back of the chair.

He'll never want to walk. He'll make me run for him. She softened, thinking of how he had liked to dance. He was a really good dancer. He was always hard to get along with, but he really could dance, she thought approvingly. It had been a long time since there was a good wedding where they had danced together. Mostly, he danced with Maria. Or Gina. Now Maria was dead, and Gina had run away. He was angry all the time, over everything and nothing. Now, she thought dryly, he's all mine! The bitterness, the anger, it's all for me. She followed the orderly, who wheeled him into his room and began to unpack his things. Now that he was here, she would be here. That was the right thing to do.

Day after day she came to the light-green room to sit by him. When she tried to talk, he turned away. When she told him stories, he didn't listen. When she came late, he was furious, and if she wanted to leave before eight at night, he grew enraged. So she sat without speaking, bringing him water, changing the TV channel, talking with the other patients, until the doctors brought his diabetes under control. But by the time they did, Dr. Ginori had gone to a convention in Texas and Dr. Timo, his young assistant, operated. Laura didn't know exactly how it happened. Either Ginori had not told Timo what to do or Timo thought he knew better. These hotshot kids always think they know better! Timo had tried to transplant arteries, first from Nino's other leg—the one they called the good one—and then from his arm. Nino's heart began to fail, and it was so difficult just to keep him alive that all they could do was sew up what they had done. They didn't get around to removing the gangrened foot. So now, Laura explained to anyone who would listen, the diabetes is haywire again, his heart is bad, his other leg and arm may go, and he still has gangrene.

"I would like to kill that doctor," Laura cried. "If I had known that Dr. Timo was going to do that, I would never have made Nino sign the release.

"Look," Dr. Timo had said, "I worked all night to keep him alive. I'm not in the business of hurting people. I just thought that so long as there was a chance of saving the leg, we should try it. He would be gone now if it weren't for me."

"Do you think he isn't gone, the way you left him?" Laura demanded.

"The issue," Dr. Timo insisted, "is what we will do now. We're going to let him regain his strength, let his heart stabilize, and bring the diabetes under control."

"You can't remove the gangrene until his condition stabilizes, and it's hard to control the condition while he has the gangrene," Laura said. "You're full of doubletalk. What you mean is, it's a question whether his heart or the gangrene kills him first. You know what you did?" Laura said, poking him in the chest with her finger. "You put him in a contest!"

Dr. Timo gave up. "Don't ask me to do anything again."

"I didn't ask you to do anything in the first place. Did I ask him?" Laura looked toward the sky. "No," she said, "I didn't. I asked Ginori. Why he has you for an assistant is beyond me."

Dr. Timo walked away.

Laura sat down, still muttering. Even when you won, you lost. He was just a hotshot, a kid. He even looked about fourteen years old. Thinks he can fix anything. But she shouldn't have talked to him that way. Why not? she demanded. He makes a mistake and I pay for it. Why did it always have to happen that way? Maybe it's my fault, she thought. I came here so he could get better treatment. Things go better in a good hospital! No matter how hard she tried to learn the way things ran, the world always got the best of her. Rizelli would have cut off his foot without trying to do anything else. He wouldn't have known how. She wondered if he were even licensed to do surgery. He wouldn't have looked further than a small operation and a fee. When she thought she was being smart—protecting Nino from that dirty hospital—she had led him straight to this. They even had the papers against her. She had told him to sign the release after Ginori had explained the operation he would do—just the gangrene. But the papers didn't say anything about that. When you say yes, she thought, you say yes to everything.

She shook her head and stared, not at him—he was too bruised and swollen even to look at—but at the monitors that blipped his heartbeat. It was hard being alone like this. The more she was with him, she knew, the more alone she felt. But now it was worse. She missed Gina. Not that she was any help, but at least you could talk to her. She could never talk to Nino about anything. Her friends were all right, but there were things you couldn't tell a friend. Her neighbors? Agnes, the eyeball, the busybody? Every time someone gave a party she showed up for a cookie and a glass of something. This morning on my way to the hospital, she stopped me to ask where I'm going. What business is it of hers? Laura had sworn she wouldn't call Gina, even though she had received Gina's note with the two telephone numbers. She knew what the other number meant. But maybe now that he was dying it didn't matter. The gravity of the situation hit. The bleeps kept up on the screen, but glancing at his swollen, feverish, bruised body, she couldn't see how they could go on bleeping. She rummaged in her bag for change for the phone.

Alex hadn't deserved the unkind things Molly had said about him. He was in love, and love was loosening him. Gina had changed a lot of things for him, he thought, looking at her. He couldn't get over the idea of her giving up everyone for him. He had never felt so good about himself; never so much in tune with his friends or equal to his father. She didn't have the corrosive kind of independence that made girls like Molly so hard. She didn't seem to have any strong impulses apart from the one that had driven her toward him and away from her parents. She was lovely, he thought. And he would do right by her. Maybe he would go back to school. He would finish.

"It's funny," he said to Gina, "how loving you changes things. I feel closer to everyone because I'm close to you and I don't think the world is such an angry place."

"What a wonderful thing to say," she said, looking at him. He had a way of irritating her one minute and then coming out of nowhere with a warmth that always overpowered her.

She was so unformed, he thought. She drank up everything he showed her. She had her own ideas, but never said anything that contradicted his. What interested him interested her. She took up what he said and carried it further, coming up with angles he had never considered. He felt a rush of feeling for her.

"Don't you feel the same way?" he said. "I think sometimes that I've just come out of solitary."

"Not exactly," she said. "I feel closer to you than ever, but . . . " she let her voice trail off. It was hard to say that she hadn't thought she would feel so confined. Loving him had set her apart or against just about everyone she had ever known or cared for. She had begun to envy a little the other people at school who weren't rushing for a job every day and had time to hang around and talk. It was definitely not like getting out of solitary, she thought. More like getting into it.

"You feel," he said, finishing her sentence, "afraid of having thrown in with me." He put his arms around her and began stroking her face. "You think I'll go, but I won't go," he said in a soft voice. "You think I'll never do anything, but I will do something. You think I'll stop loving you, but I won't stop loving you."

He held her suspended under his sing-song voice, stopping the dry thoughts that flashed through her mind, even though her fears were not the ones he named. He began licking her eyelids. "Don't," she said. "It feels funny and anyway I want to see. I can't see when you do that."

"You don't have to see anything," he said. "I'll . . . "

She interrupted. "You're going to say you'll see for me; you'll see a better world, you'll see," she started to laugh, "a higher beauty."

He backed off. "Are you making fun of me?" he said uncertainly. She could be cutting, he remembered. He didn't mind that—she could be terribly funny about other people, and harsh in her judgments. He supposed that had enabled her to come to him, and, he foresaw, would keep her loyal to him no matter what anyone said. She would simply cut them down. But so far her bite had been for everybody else, not for him. He didn't doubt that her will would never confront his; she wasn't like that. But her tongue was another matter.

"I'm not making fun of you," she said, finally. She hugged him and began to stroke his back. "It's probably better to see everything through you." She pressed her face into his chest. My God, she thought. I'll say anything now. He kissed her and they lay down, slipping out of their clothes on the way to the bed. They lay pressed against each other. His skin felt like sunlight on a warm summer day, a loosening, silken heat. There was nothing like getting lost in it, the great wash of tenderness and urgency that seemed to flow out of his touch.

The phone rang. "Ignore it," he said.

She didn't answer, but the telephone rang and rang. It seemed to ring for hours, until, unnerved, he picked it up. He listened for a moment and handed it to Gina.

"Where are you when I need you?" Laura demanded.

"What do you need me for?" Gina asked, upset by Laura's voice here in the room. It didn't seem right to be undressed while she spoke to her.

"I need you," Laura said, "to keep me company while your father dies. Do you think I would call you if it wasn't important?"

"No," Gina said, "I don't. Where are you?"

"University Hospital, fourteenth floor."

"I'll be right there." She hung up, forgetting Alex for a moment, looking absently for her sneakers.

"What's that about?" said Alex irritably, sitting up in bed.

"My father's dying; my mother said to come."

"Where is he?" Alex asked.

"University Hospital."

"How do you know he's really dying? What's he dying of? He didn't seem that sick when I saw him."

"I don't know. She didn't say, but she wouldn't tell me he was dying if she didn't believe he was dying. It's not the kind of thing she would do."

"You don't know what she would do. She's never been in a situation like this with you before. Maybe she just wants to get you back."

"It's not that far," Gina said. "She's waiting for me. How can I not go?" she asked bluntly.

"Well, when you left, you left. Did they care what happened to you? They can't just phone in the middle of the night and expect you to run when they behaved the way they did. I don't think you have to drop everything."

Gina looked at him. She began to put on her clothes. "You're really mad, aren't you?"

"You get up when we're in the middle of something. The dishes are still on the table from dinner. And you're ready to walk out. Just like that. What about me?" Alex complained.

"What about you? You can find something to do. Keep busy, read a book. Better yet, wash the dishes."

"I don't see why you can't go later or in the morning," Alex persisted.

He doesn't really expect me not to go now, Gina thought. He just wants to be apologized to, reassured that he's more important than anyone. It was ridiculous. The more committed he was to her, the more he seemed to expect her to revolve around him. He had a way of accusing her of not feeling or doing enough for him that upset her. At times she felt she was on a treadmill, trying to please someone who refused to be pleased. At other times, she just wanted to get away from the tension and anxiety he aroused.

Still, Alex had a point. Nino and Laura had ignored her since she left. And now Laura asks: Where are you when I need you? Where was *she* when I needed her? Always kowtowing to Nino. She was there for me all the same, Gina acknowledged. As much as she could be. It was insane to think otherwise.

"Well," Alex demanded.

Gina pulled on her sweater and sat down on the bed.

"Alex," she said dryly, caressing his cheek, "when you're dying, you can come first, too."

"OK, OK," he said, beginning to look sheepish. "Come back as soon as you can."

Gina rose and walked to the door. "I'll see you later." She closed the door behind her. As soon as she was in the hallway, she began to run. She ran to Fourteenth Street and Avenue B and started walking west to First Avenue. She saw the bus coming and ran for it.

"What took you so long?" Laura asked when she got there.

"I came as soon as I could," Gina said.

"Well, I'm glad to see you. I'm glad you came. Look at him. I feel it's all my fault," she said, breaking down. "I took him here to get decent treatment and look what happened."

"Can he hear us?" Gina asked.

"Who knows?"

"Dad," Gina said, moving next to him. "Do you know we're here? Can you hear anything?" His sheets were stained with blood; his arms were wired, one to an IV bottle, the other to the monitoring equipment. He made no sign.

"Let's go outside for a minute," Laura said. "I didn't want to say this in front of him," Laura said in the corridor, "but that's how they look when they go."

"Did they tell you he was dying?"

"They say a lot of things. They're worse than the weather bureau."

"It wasn't your fault," Gina said. "You did the right thing. How could you know in advance that this would happen?"

"He doesn't look to me like he'll come out of here alive. I'm going to wait here. You sit there," she said, pointing to the other end of the bench.

"Did you have anything to eat?" Gina said.

"No," Laura said. "Go and get me something, will you? There's a delicatessen across the street." Laura handed her some money.

Gina walked into the elevator, dreading the long night in the waiting room. What if he did die? There was so much bad feeling between them. That almost made it harder if he died now. He can't die. He won't die, she corrected. Not with so much unfinished business. It wouldn't be like him. She paid for the sandwiches and bought a bottle of red wine with a screw cap.

"You forgot cups," Laura said. "And the nurses here don't knock themselves out getting things for you."

She was right. It took Gina a while before she found an aide who would bother getting her some paper cups.

"Red," Laura said appreciatively. "It's the best thing for the blood." She sipped quietly for a moment. "If he doesn't die, he'll be crippled." She took a bite of the sandwich. "Salami, Genoa salami," she noted. "What can I say. It's just my luck. He always wrecked my luck," Laura said. "You know, when I was pregnant my mother got very sick from a heart attack. I made a novena to Saint Anthony and promised to name my baby after him if she got better. Well, she got better and when you were born I intended to name you Antoinette. But in those days they kept you in the hospital for ten days. While I was laid up, your father went to City Hall and had your name registered as Gina, after his mother. After I had promised you to Saint Anthony. I was furious. What if my mother had gotten sick again because I hadn't kept my word?" She took another bite of the sandwich. "They put too much pepper in this salami," she remarked. "To make a long story short, I had to get up out of bed and go to City Hall to try to change the name and pay to have it done legally. A week or two old and a baby with legal fees because of him," she said, gesturing toward Nino.

"Did your mother get better after that?" Gina asked.

"Of course," Laura said. "But no thanks to him. He went and changed it back. I never forgave him for that. I shouldn't speak ill of him in his condition." She crossed herself and took another sip of wine.

"I don't know why," Gina said. "He's not dead yet, and there's plenty of time to look at his good qualities later on."

"He was always very loyal," Laura said.

"He isn't dead yet."

"Well," Laura admitted, "it's probably not right to speak ill of the sick, either. But after all, you have to say something. I remember in a situation like this Concetta promised to walk on her knees all the way to the Church of Saint Jude. Well," Laura considered, "I never had much to do with Saint Jude. And given what your father did to Saint Anthony, I doubt that he would care. He is forgiving, though," she said.

She never rules anything out completely, Gina thought, amused. She would take him to the best hospital she could think of, but then she would cast around for the right saint, just to be sure. But it all goes wrong in the end, anyway.

"What if he wakes up?" Gina asked. "Do you think it would be worse if he knew I was here? He never has much to say to me, anyway."

"He'll talk to you when he's ready to talk to you," Laura said. "It doesn't matter that you . . . ," she groped for a neutral word. "It makes no difference," she concluded. "It's true you don't get along, but who does he get along with? Now he just mopes around. He wasn't even getting angry anymore, the way he used to. When he first got the fever, I thought he was just blue."

"I don't think there was much you could do once it started." Gina said. "It's not like an infection from the outside. It came from his own system."

"It came from the slow blood," Laura agreed quickly. She poured Gina another cup of wine. "How are you doing in school?"

"OK. It's interesting. Everyone is running around, doing things. There's a lot going on," she said wistfully.

"You have time to do homework and do things too, what with working every day?" Laura asked.

"Yes," Gina lied.

"I wish you'd meet someone else," Laura said. "You know

we'll be here all night." She looked into the room at the monitoring screen. "Does *he* know you'll be here all night?" she asked Gina.

"No," Gina admitted. "I thought I'd be back soon."

"You better call him or he'll worry."

"He won't worry."

"Call him," Laura said, handing her some change.

She took the money and went to a phone, but there was no answer.

"He's out," she said, returning.

"Out? It's almost midnight."

"He's out," Gina repeated. "Sometimes he stays out until three or four."

"He runs around?" Laura asked.

"No. He stays up talking with his friends."

"Arthur would never do that. I'm sure he doesn't know anyone who stays up that late. And when I think how good he is to his mother. How a man treats his mother is how he'll treat you. Arthur would never stay out just to talk to his friends. Do they play cards?"

"No. They just talk or walk around."

"What can they talk about for so long?"

"This and that," Gina said, amused. "What else?"

"Arthur never had that much to say. A man who keeps talking like that, you can't trust," Laura said.

"Why not?" Gina asked.

"Because he's wasting his time. If he has something on his mind, he should do something about it. If he thinks, it should be for his work. If it's for his work, he should be making use of it. If he's not making use of himself, then"—she waved her hands—"he's just an idler. If he's an idler," she concluded, "he's not for you. Your father said you would come back when you saw he was right."

"He probably thinks I'm an idler too," Gina said.

"No, he doesn't think that," Laura said flatly. "He thinks you're a sneak and a plotter, and that you can't make up your mind. Because you can't make up your mind, he thinks there's something wrong with your character. But he doesn't think you're an idler," she continued reassuringly. "He thinks you want that boy because you think he's one of them. But he says you'll find out he isn't one of them either, and since he isn't one of us, you'll be left stranded."

"He really thinks ahead, doesn't he?" Gina said, glancing at the blipping monitor.

"He always thought a lot," Laura agreed. "But the more he thought, the madder he'd get. Now he doesn't think and he doesn't get mad. He just . . ."—she paused—"sits."

"I think I'll try to call again," Gina said, getting up. She felt bad, so bad she couldn't separate all the reasons she had for being down. It was Nino going, it was Laura looking so forlorn that brought her down. It was making Alex angry. Why was it hard for him to be a good sport? What else could she have done when Laura called. He had hit her where she hurt, in her fear that she really didn't care enough. The trouble was, she must care, or his words couldn't sting her the way they did. She was angry and anxious at the same time. The phone kept ringing and ringing. It was 2:30 A.M.

Why does he have to make himself unreachable? she wondered. For all she knew he was there, not bothering to pick up the phone. Whatever she did, he never stopped raising the demands he made. They were unsatisfiable because they kept changing and ascending. His need for her to be everything, his softness, was as effective as a shotgun. At least with Nino you knew where you stood. You did what he wanted or he blew up. His needs turned the house into a shambles, but didn't seep into your soul. He didn't put anxiety and panic in your heart. She had gotten hooked into Alex's tenderness and because of it, she was going to hurt more than ever.

Alex had given up nothing. His life, in fact, was cozier than before. She had somehow cemented his friendships; his parents thought she would press him to finish school. But there he was, throwing himself in her way. "You think I'm crude, insensitive," Nino had accused her. "But let me tell you, if I'm blunt it's because I know what's right and I don't waste time fuzzying the truth. I put my cards on the table; you play the game or not." She had thought the point wasn't playing any game, but all the things that happened between moves. She was tired of everything being as black-and-white as Nino said. What really counts, she told herself, is texture and depth. Alex has that, she thought dryly. He has too much depth. She was beginning to lose her way in him. He knew how to make her feel obliged to make up for whatever his life lacked. She sat down heavily on the bench next to Laura, who was staring at the screen.

"No change," she said to Gina. "Nothing new. Is he back?"

"No," Gina said.

They sat in silence.

"So you're still here?" they heard behind them. Turning, Gina saw Alex walking toward them. He shook his head. "I couldn't believe you'd still be here."

"Where else would she be?" Laura asked pointedly. Alex blushed.

Gina felt a rush of tenderness. He had regretted what he had said to her.

Laura looked at the two of them and said nothing. Troubles come in bundles.

"It's been hours since you left," Alex reminded Gina.

"What did you expect?" Laura said wearily. "He doesn't always make a quick decision."

"Who?"

"Him," Laura said, pointing up.

"Relax," Gina said. "Let Alex keep us company if he wants to."

"I don't think that's what he came for. Is that what you want?" Laura asked.

"I'll stay for a while," he said uncomfortably.

"You know," Laura said earnestly, "I don't have anything personal against you. The reason I don't want you around is that you ruined our family."

"You're very upset," Alex said soothingly.

"Of course I'm upset," Laura answered. "Only an idiot wouldn't be upset at a time like this. My daughter runs away, my husband is dying. I would be out of my mind if that didn't upset me."

"Somehow I don't think he'll die now," Gina said.

"To tell you the truth," Laura said, "I'm beginning to think he isn't ready to leave. I thought he was, before, but he looks less and less the way they do when they go."

"Then why are you sitting here all night?" Gina asked. "Why don't we go home and come back tomorrow?"

"Because he expects it," Laura said. "It wouldn't be right to go."

Gina moved into the room so she could see him directly instead of through the window. His color was better. He looked less gray than before. Alex came up behind her and stood beside the bed, looking down.

"He does look really bad," he murmured, chastened. "Why don't you ask a doctor how he is? You can stay if you want to, but if he's going to survive, it's better to come back when he's conscious."

"She won't leave," Gina said.

"That's her decision," Alex answered.

"I can't leave her alone."

"I can't stay all night," he said.

"I can't go with you. Not now."

Whether it was their voices that roused him or just that he had turned some corner back to life, Nino opened his eyes. He gazed up through what seemed like a thick film and made out the bristling yellow outline of Alex's beard.

Gina reached for his hand. "Can you see me?" she said softly. "It's Gina."

He gripped her hand weakly, his clawlike nails brushing her wrist. He looked at her. Her eyes filled with tears. Blinking them back, she could see him study her face, then shift his eyes to Alex. He murmured something. She leaned closer to hear, the tears falling down her cheeks, onto his pillow. He was murmuring the same words over and over. At first she couldn't make out what they were. "He's speaking Italian," she said. "Go call Laura." She pressed her face toward him. And she heard, finally, the round, smooth syllables he had been murmuring like a litany: *"Putana, putana, putana. . . ."*

"I'll see you tomorrow," she said, releasing his hand.

She brushed past her mother. "He'll be OK," she said as Laura went past her to the bed. She walked so rapidly down the hall that Alex had trouble catching up.

"What did he tell you? Was it about me?" Alex demanded.

"No," she snapped.

"Are you coming home now?"

Gina kept walking. "He's not going to die," she said. "He's too angry to die. He'll live for years, just on his self-righteousness."

"What did he say?" Alex demanded, pleased by her bitterness.

"It's none of your business," she answered.

"Tell me," he insisted. "Did he ask you to stay and you refused? Was it something like that?"

"No," she said. "It wasn't like that at all."

"Well, what was it?" he said peevishly. "I couldn't hear anything."

"It's not supposed to be a radio program, you know. There's supposed to be some privacy about deathbed words."

"But you said it's not his deathbed," he pursued, rushing to keep pace with her. "This has kept me up all night and I have a right to know."

Gina stopped. "What he did," she said, looking him in the eye, "was call me a whore."

Alex laughed. "He really hangs on, doesn't he?" he said appreciatively. "He really hangs on."

She looked at him. Had he come to keep her company, or had he come to see if she were really there?

Six

"When your number's up, it's up. And when it's not, it's not," said Nino's nephew Vinnie. "Remember how they always called you last? Remember the position tryouts for the Falcons? You missed so many chances to make it, the season was over and you never even got up. Remember?" Vinnie said.

"Not as well as you do," Nino said. "Why don't you cheer me up and tell me about my wins?"

"I got less to think about than you," Vinnie said, ignoring the advice. "That's why my memory is so good. I go here and there," he waved his hand. "Somehow there's no time to think." It occurred to him that Nino would never get up again. "It was never my talent, like it was yours," Vinnie said, trying to make amends for Nino's immobility.

"It isn't how much you think," Nino said sagely, "it's what you think."

"How was it, the operation?" Vinnie asked, eager to change the subject.

"One minute the doctor says to me, 'Raise your leg.' So I

try to raise it. Then he says, 'Raise the other one.' That's the last thing I remember. Next thing I know, they're both gone."

"Just like that," Vinnie said, shaking his head. "Well, the important thing is that now you'll get better."

"Better than what?" Nino asked wryly.

"Better than you were."

"Oh, you don't get better from this," Nino said emphatically. "When you're damned, you're damned." He looked at Vinnie, offended that he had slighted his illness.

"I wouldn't say damned, Nino. You're not damned. You're an amputee, but you're not damned."

"It's a question of what comes first."

"The diabetes came first," Vinnie said, misunderstanding him. "Then the gangrene, and then the amputation. How could there be any doubt about that? Look at Antonetta's son." Vinnie gestured vaguely. "You know."

"I know," Nino said. "Laura thinks I don't know, but I know even though I'm not in the family."

"Funny, isn't it," Vinnie said. "How everybody knew but him. He got the diabetes too, but never took care of it, with that pot belly. At forty-nine he goes blind; two years later"—snap! went Vinnie's fingers—"he's gone. After he's dead his wife calls Amarico to tell him his brother is dead and where the funeral will be. 'He's not my brother,' Amarico says to her. 'He's my half-brother.' What was the point of telling, after he was dead. These Neapolitans are crazy."

"He was mad at his mother because she wouldn't give him the money to become a loan shark."

"She was right," Vinnie said. "He's the type who would rough up someone and wind up in jail in a business like that. It takes discipline to do that kind of work."

Nino nodded his agreement. They were overly emotional, Neapolitans. That was Laura's trouble. She kept answering when there weren't any questions. He watched her in the corner, talking with the doctor. He couldn't hear what she was saying, but he knew she was telling him what to do by the way she underlined everything she said with her hands. These Neapolitans only talk with their hands. Tie up their hands, they couldn't say a thing. He paused for a minute, amused at the possibilities.

When Gina came in, Laura joined Vinnie and Nino.

Gina nodded to Nino without saying hello. "I brought you a radio so you can listen to the ball game," she said.

"Don't tell me what I should listen to," Nino said.

"He's too sick to listen to the radio," Laura added. "Can't you see that?"

"I want the radio," Nino said. "What do you mean I'm sick?"

"I'll put it under your pillow so you know where it is. When you feel up to it, it will be there."

"How are you?" he asked Gina.

"OK," she answered. "I'm fine. Very well."

"Compared to me," he whispered, "anybody is well. How are you compared to how you were?"

"Better," she nodded. "Better than ever."

"You look lousy," Nino offered. "Your hair is too long and your clothes are too tight."

"No kidding," Gina said. "You, on the other hand, look terrific."

"Never give an inch, do you. Someday you'll learn the meaning of compassion."

"Not from you," she said.

"Why do you have to fight?" Laura asked. "Isn't there enough trouble without that?"

"Yeah," Vinnie said. "Especially in front of me. You know," he said to Gina, "you should show more respect for your relatives."

"I meant no offense to you, Cousin Vinnie," Gina said. "Don't take it that way."

"If you don't want me to take it that way, then don't be so fresh to your father after all he's been through," Vinnie said piously.

He had her there. No one could deny it was terrible. Nino's face had aged, she noticed, about a thousand years.

"I didn't come to argue," Gina said. "I just came to see how he was." What was the point of trying to defend herself? If she claimed Nino had started the trouble, Vinnie would only say she provoked him by everything she was doing. It was better to let it drop.

"I'm glad to see you're looking better," she said to Nino.

"Well, now you have a father with no legs. You don't have to worry about being followed," he said, eyeing her.

What was she supposed to say? Why did he always have to set traps? "You'll find a way." She forced a grin.

"You're right. I'm glad you know that." He pressed back into his pillows. He seemed suddenly exhausted by everyone. He began to speak to Vinnie again, in rapid dialect she couldn't fully catch.

"Let him rest," Vinnie said. "He needs his sleep." He ushered them away from the bed. "You better come back tomorrow," he said to Gina.

"See that you do," Nino called. "See that you do."

The operation, Laura thought, is simple. Cut and saw and stitch; nothing complicated about this surgery. It just complicated everything about your life, she frowned, wheeling Nino from the hospital door where the nurse had left him. They cut and stitch and send you home. Then you have to live with what they've done for the rest of your life.

When the pin came loose that had fastened the left leg of

Nino's pants, Laura said, "I told him so. You can't pin pants so they stay up when you move around."

"Who did you tell?" Nino asked without interest.

"That doctor. He told me to wrap them like a blanket around each stump."

Nino said nothing all the way home. This would be the only way he could go anywhere now. In a van for wheelchairs. The trip back to Queens through the Midtown Tunnel made him even gloomier. Not even the view from the Queensboro Bridge to cheer him up, he thought bleakly. When they got home, Laura took his pants from the closet and made a pile of them. She measured the stumps while he lay back, cursing her under his breath. She measured each pants leg and cut off most of it.

"What you've got left," she said to him, "is eleven inches on each side."

He turned over. "Leave me alone. Don't tell me such things. I can still feel them there, both of them."

She looked at him. He never had much sense of reality. She sat hemming next to his bed to keep him company. In an hour or so she finished. She took the cuffs and bottoms she had cut off. None of them would make really good dust rags. Nevertheless, she slit them, cut them into rectangles, and folded them into a pile. Nino started to cry.

"Why do you do this in front of me?" he said.

"There is no point in crying over what's gone. None at all. Now at least you'll look neat."

"Madonna mia," he murmured.

"After all, even she can't bring back your legs." Then she added as an afterthought, "You could have prayed to Saint Anthony if you hadn't offended him. Now it's too late. He wouldn't answer your prayers."

"Why didn't *you* pray to him? You think you've got some kind of hotline."

"Don't be sarcastic. You were never willing to offer anything. Concetta promised to crawl on her knees from Mulberry Street to his church. Antonetta gave up bread for a year. You wouldn't even name your child after him to save my mother's life. Every time I think of that it burns me up."

"That was years ago."

"It doesn't matter. What's right is right."

"Why do you add to my suffering, my misfortune?" he said, drawing out the syllables pathetically and pointing to his stumps.

That was the trouble with Sicilians, Laura thought. They brood. All the time. When something really goes wrong, they brood so much they can't come back. Thank God I'm not one of them. "Your misfortune is what it is," Laura said. "It is my misfortune too. The sooner we both accept that, the better off we'll be. Maybe I could pray to Saint Anthony now. I thought in your case he wouldn't listen. But maybe now," she said, letting his grayness have its impact on her, "he would."

"I don't want any help from that bastard!" Nino said.

Laura stared at him. "You," she said, pointing at him emphatically, "are hopeless."

"That's right," he agreed. "Bring me lunch." He pounded the bed. "Bring it here. I'm not getting up today."

"You should move around," Laura said. "If you don't you're liable to get gangrene in the stumps and go through this all over again. You have to try to keep your circulation up."

"I'm not getting up. And I'm hungry. Bring it here and bring it now!" he said.

She walked into the kitchen. "A hell of a lot you care if I have to shorten everything again," she flung at him over her shoulder.

He turned the television set on, making it as loud as possible.

"More baseball!" Laura yelled. "That's all you care about." After a while, she brought him a huge plate of spaghetti with meat sauce and two breaded veal cutlets, placed on a tin bed tray with a pattern of peaches and grapes painted on it. She went back into the kitchen and called Wilson Surgical Equipment to price a hospital bed for him.

"It's eight hundred dollars if you buy it, and six hundred dollars per month if you rent it," the salesman said.

"That's an enormous rental," Laura said. The price of everything connected with his illness had already passed beyond her imagination. "Why would anybody rent at that price when in two months it costs more than it would to buy it?"

"Because Medicare pays for the rental, but they won't pay for the purchase of a bed," the salesman said.

"That can't be right."

"It is. I know better than you, lady, I do this all the time. Let me know when you're ready."

"When could you have it here?" Laura said, giving her address.

"We deliver in Queens on Tuesdays and Thursdays. I can get it to you the Tuesday after you place the order."

"I'll think about it," she said. Although what was there to think about? If you need something, you need it. It was just so hard to say you would rent something for more than it was worth, even if you weren't paying for it with your own money. Well, it was your money, in taxes. You spend all your life watching every cent, and being careful, and you get into a position where you're forced to waste. It was one thing after another. The more you tried to do the right thing, the more you were taken advantage of. Sometimes, she thought, I lose all my ambition. The kitchen floor, she noticed, hadn't been cleaned in days. Either she had been in the hospital visiting him, or was too tired from the trip. She took a mop from its place behind the refrigerator and filled a bucket with water and Mr. Clean. She took out a foam pad for her knees for the places the mop wouldn't reach. She made sharp-smelling puddles on the floor, leaning over them without moving her brush. She began to scrub under the kitchen table. When she had washed her way to the door, she took off her shoes and put on a pair of socks so she wouldn't make footprints on the wet floor.

"Take away the dishes," Nino yelled over the noise of the ball game. Laura went into his room and took his empty plates back toward the kitchen. He watched her.

"What's on your feet?" he demanded.

"Socks."

"Those are my socks," he said.

"I thought," she stammered, "since you didn't need them anymore, I could use them."

"What's the matter with you, taking my socks? Give them back to me."

"What for? We can't afford to waste, you know. It isn't cheap, buying medicine and food."

"I'll eat the socks."

She took them off.

"Put them back."

"They're wet. I can't put them in a drawer."

"Hang them where I can see them," he ordered.

She hung them over the back of a chair and walked out of the room.

"How quickly you can walk away from me," he muttered.

"I'm going shopping," she said. "I need fruit."

"You can't leave now. What if I need something?" he implored.

She looked at him. "All right," she said, "I'll stay. But I

have to go out sometime. I can't stay here always just in case you want a glass of water."

"I'll tell you when you can go," he said quietly. But he knew that when he fell asleep, as he always did now after eating, she would leave. The prospect of her waiting for him to fall asleep kept him up for an extra hour and a half. My vigil, he thought to himself. My watchful eye! But the effort at sight cost him more each moment. My baleful glance, he thought dreamily, as Laura peeked in once again to see if he was out yet. I'm the evil eye—the thought flitted through his slowing brain and made him smile into the sleep he couldn't keep off another moment.

His wakefulness cast a shadow over everything. It proved he had weight. How funny his balefulness seemed, though, as he reached through sleep. He seemed to travel now, losing bitterness as he went, losing even the sting of what he had lost as he reached another side of memory. He was reaching it now. He could smell the sun-warmed juniper, the sea spray, the homecoming place. He knew that soon when he went there he would meet Maria. The villagers would be there: Fabio and his father, Enrico, would be arguing. His mother would be crocheting at the window, yards of bedspreads spilling from her lap in a pattern of roses and grape leaves, all in ivory silk thread. So far it was still a swept and brilliant openness he reached through sleep. He could see the craggy cliffs full of shadow and light; the sun playing across the pitted surface like a comforting hand. He had been sure he would grow up to be like the cliffs, worn and constant. Now they took him in, the craggy emptiness swelling on every side like an embrace. So far his sleep had been all flight, warmth, and return, the precarious rocks like a cradle to his age. But he feared more and more the certain day when sleep would bring him a welcoming committee.

When Gina came in he was in an almost breathless sleep.

She sat down, without bothering to take off her jacket, at the folding card table Laura had put near the bed. The gray bareness of the room hit her with as much force as his ashen face. I never realized how bad it was, she thought. All those years, it was just a room. She had never been in a room, she realized, that wasn't just a place to put a bed and a chest until she left him. Not, she thought wryly, that she had one herself. But she saw they existed; they had warmth, light, color, a personal stamp. It wasn't just that Nino had no money. It is, she thought, *his* personal stamp, this grayness. The muddy gray-beige of the walls, the faded ninon curtains, the wooden slat blinds, the pitted walls, painted over and over but never plastered and smoothed, the floor scarred with metal roller skate wheels, the streak where the sewing machine had been dragged to be taken out and motorized. The lamp with the thick globe, bought on sale, but no bargain for it shed almost no light, the heavy crucifix over the bed, the plasticized diplomas, the picture of Cardinal Spellman—the list swelling in her mind began to produce the familiar homecoming feeling, the solid anger she only wanted to flee.

Only by flight could you hope to leave it behind, she thought. It was a thing, that anger, an object like the plasticized diplomas, the crucifix that had hung over her grandmother's coffin—the list beginning again couldn't be silenced; the things seemed to speak for themselves. How much distance does it take to stop hearing them? All he had done was lie there sleeping, and he had already exhausted her, she thought. Still another easy victory. She looked around restlessly. She would wait. If he didn't wake up in half an hour, she would write a note and leave. What could she say? Write a note: Dear Dad, Came but you were out. Ha ha. Or, Dear Dad, Brought you some oil and vinegar. Given your vegetable state, it seemed the perfect gift. . . . She was disgusted with herself just for thinking that. He was right.

She was terrible. It was the sense of disturbance she couldn't get rid of, and the stale anger he brought out in her. That was what made her nasty, she thought, edging away from the issue. There it is, getting angry makes you want to run from it; but anger exhausts, and cuts your stamina so you can't.

The trouble was lack of sleep. Every time she fell asleep since she had seen him at the hospital, livid and bruised in his bed, wired to machines and tubes, she had dreamed of him as he was when she was little. She would see him throwing a ball, ready to play catch with her as though she were a boy. The day the hard baseball hit her in the nose—she could feel the impact in her sleep. She remembered when she was five and she and her friend were playing in the empty lot near the church. They had found cans filled with hardened cement. They had tried to get the cement out, like a stone mud pie. When she had picked up the can it had fallen on her foot and her foot had swelled up like a balloon. She yowled with pain as she hobbled into the house. He had been home and he bound the foot in a splint made of Popsicle sticks and gauze. He packed it with ice in a towel and carried her to the doctor. By then she had been screaming at him—"It's not that bad! Let me go! Let me down!" But he was convinced it was broken, and wouldn't put her down until it had been X-rayed. He carried her for blocks, holding her so tightly she scarcely had air enough to screech and breathe at the same time. She dreamed that over and over, always without any sense of how he had meant to protect her. Always the sense of being held and trapped, the fear that anything wrong with her meant she would be stuck forever.

Why can't I get over that, she thought. After all, he's the cripple now. But in her nights he still seemed to hold her in a grip she couldn't break. She was beginning to sweat. She turned away from him, stepping through the clutter of wastebaskets and snack tables to stare out the window into the alley. She sat on the sill, pulling her feet up onto it, fitting herself into the window frame, staring at the gray wall. She had learned something about herself, learned that she was hooked on the act of leaving. It felt good. Escape was reassurance, was possibility, was avoiding entrapment. Even in the good times with Alex, she saw the trip back to her own place—a room as shabby as this one—as only a stopover to other, uncertain destinations. Going excited her. She would keep doing it. But without staying with anyone, what was there that would give life meaning or shape?

She had learned to put those questions aside. She had concentrated on taking charge of her life in small pieces, parceling out the hours of each day as she saw fit. Studying anthropology she found her mental discipline seemed to grow, even if everything else became more chaotic. Nino had been right; she was calculating. The advantages she worked for weren't material or practical, but psychic gains: to connect with something strong at the center of herself, to do something so well that that center took over everything; this was what she wanted. But, she could see, looking tensely at the rough wall, it might never happen. She felt the pressure of Nino's fatalism. Was every attempt at success, every small accomplishment, just a way of moving another inch away from him? How many would it take to reach a safe distance?

Poor Nino. His grayness was so terrible she couldn't look at him. She hunched over, grasping her hands around her knees. The wholeness, the coherence, the orderliness of his life should have come to more than this terrible stability in a small room. You had to admire—she hesitated—his purity, his contempt for material things, his sense of moral obligation. How could she tell him how much he meant to her? Even the sense of reality, the practical sharpness, the toughness that seemed to set her off more and more, she had to admit, she owed to him. Of course, she wouldn't admit it, not to him. So why now, when she had never felt stronger, never less angry with him, why, every night since his legs fell away, did she encounter in her dreams images of herself in his grip, an immobilized child? Which of them was the cripple, anyway?

There she was, Nino thought, crouched like a baby in the belly staring at the alley wall. He tried to blink away the white film that seemed to be in his eyes all the time now. When she didn't know he was around, or thought he wasn't looking, her face was full of moods. As soon as he spoke to her it became fixed and brittle, just a mask. It's because she's afraid of me, Nino concluded. Well, she should be.

"If I don't talk to you, will you sit there like a stick forever? Is this the way you visit me? Is this your idea of cheering me up?" he demanded. "What's the matter with you?"

"Nothing, I'm fine. Anyway, that's what I'm supposed to ask *you*. How are you?"

"Don't change the subject. I already know how I am. You don't look fine. You look tense. Look how you're gripping your hands, how you're twisting toward me in that ridiculous position. Why don't you sit here," he ordered, pointing to the chair next to his bed. "You can jump out the window later."

"I was comfortable that way," she said, picking her way to the chair through the clutter.

"Always on edge, wanting to go, wanting to go," he grumbled. "What is that saying? A wise man is happy anywhere? Smart people don't always look, look, look for someplace else. They want what they have, and learn how to enjoy it."

"I don't think I know anybody like that," Gina said sourly. "That doesn't apply to anyone who's really alive. Being restless is being alive."

"Being restless is the worst part of being alive," Nino

corrected. "It is definitely at the bottom. It shows a lack of understanding and discipline. Your restlessness," he said meditatively, without malice, "is the lowest, most foolish kind. You keep running after happiness and pleasure. You were even foolish enough to want to live like an adult before you are one. Only an idiot . . . an afflicted person"—he corrected himself, edging away from nastiness—"would be an adult before he had to. You ran after change, you wanted to speed everything up. You know where speeding up time leads?" he asked mildly. "It leads to the end and it's a mistake to hasten the end. The right thing isn't change. It's simple, static, maybe lonely." He paused for a moment. "It's getting rid of the idea that you should be looking for anything. It's realizing that happiness is a static thing, something that happens when you feel no desire for anything tangible. It's freedom from disturbance, from wanting to move around."

Gina listened, disturbed and irritated, but moved by how he could go on. He always justified whatever condition he was in. Now that his legs were gone, immobility was in. The happiest man, she thought derisively, is the one who can't move, can't want, can't think, can't will.

"Life," Nino began winding down, "should have the fewest possible distractions. Laura!" he shouted. "Bring me coffee!"

"You shouldn't yell at her like that. And she shouldn't come like she does, like a slave."

"Don't tell me what to do," he said. "Your mother is a saint." He grinned. "I'm the occasion for her saintliness. For . . ."—his voice trailed off for a moment—". . . for her grace. She'll gain an indulgence through me. You see," he went on, "doing nothing, lying here, everything falls into place."

It's death, she thought. It's a justification for his leaving. By the time he goes he'll be able to tout it as the best, the rightest thing to do.

"Look at you. You want this, you want that, you want them. You think you'll find something better than me." He leaned over shakily. "You listen to me. You are restless and you are a woman. That combination is a disease. And that disease has symptoms. You have will, that's a symptom. But you lack discipline. And will without discipline isn't going to bring you anything but misery. You'll make one mistake after another. You'll suffer," he said, his voice becoming tearful. "You'll suffer. Let me tell you," he said, his long yellowed fingers closing around her hand, "there is no cure for what you've got."

"Why does every conversation have to turn into an attack on me?" Gina said, choking up.

"Because . . ." he began, but his voice broke. Why did he bother? He couldn't answer anymore. Somehow all his weakness was rolled up into her! She had been so lovely, so gentle, laughing all the time since she was a baby. He had thought the world was too rough for her. Now look at her, just a tramp. She couldn't even keep her legs together. She had to go off with that—the word exploded the pictures of her he carried in his mind: the starched pinafores, the white dresses. He could see her in her white silk blouse, with Alex unbuttoning it.

"You bitch," he muttered. "You filthy bitch."

She looked at him impassively.

"That doesn't bother you, does it?" he said, half rising from his bed, his skin gray against the white sheets.

"It bothers me. It bothers me. There's nothing I can say to it. I can't even take in all you say. You go from one mood to another."

"You take it all in," he accused her. "Don't play dumb with me."

"I can't get all it means," she murmured.

"Don't talk back to me," he said, clenching his fists into the sheets.

"Look," she said, "don't get upset. You want me to leave?"

"You like the idea, don't you. Can't wait to get away. Well, you can damn well stay here. I feel like talking and I can't talk to your mother because she never keeps quiet."

"I thought she was a saint."

"She is." He grinned. "A Neapolitan saint is a noisy saint. You think I like everything quiet in its place because I'm afraid of life. But you're wrong. It's because I like to protect things. Whenever you change something, you make it worse. That's true regardless of what you intend. Even if you want to do something right, you wind up with the wrong thing if you interfere with the way things are.

"When I was a boy in Ventimiglia, there was a girl everybody in the village loved. She was a schoolteacher—young, sweet, kind. She was only nineteen when she got sick with cholera and died. While she was dying, she said goodbye to all her friends and she asked them to bury her with her father. Because everyone loved her, they tried to outdo themselves when she died in doing what she had wanted. Now, her father had died the year before," Nino said, getting into his story. "But the carpenter, to please her, built an oversize coffin. The priest agreed to bless it. Everyone went to the cemetery to bring back her father, to . . . reunite Lucia with her father. They opened up his coffin. It was a summer day. You could smell the lemon trees," he said, his voice trailing off for a moment. "We all stood watching while the carpenter worked on the lid. He raised it up. It was a miracle! There was her father, looking perfectly alive! Everything was the same, nothing decayed after a whole year." He waved his hand over Gina. He could see she hung on every word. He passed his hand above her, as if in benediction.

"We crossed ourselves," Nino continued, "marveling at the perfection of his body. Even the priest thought God had offered him a chance to see His work. I was only a little boy, but he clasped my hand and said something about the power of the resurrection. The strength of love! Lucia must have known he would be like this. But as we crossed ourselves for the third time, Lucia's father fell to dust. Everything—the skin that had seemed so perfect—all fell into dust! I was only a boy," Nino repeated, "but I remember as if it were this morning, as if it were only a moment ago that I ran there, and saw it, and saw the face fall into nothing."

Nino and Gina, spellbound, looked at each other. He had the gift of taking her out of herself. He caught her up in his stories. It made her uncomfortable, but it was undeniable: she couldn't ward off his spell.

"What happened then?" Gina asked softly, afraid he might not go on.

"Then," Nino continued, "Ignazio, the butcher, said, 'It's a shame to put a beautiful girl in with a skeleton,' and shook his head.

"The priest was upset too. It wasn't, you know, strictly right to have disturbed the grave. They only did it because of how much they loved Lucia. The priest must have thought that God let them witness His miracle, and maybe Lucia's father fell to dust to remind us we should have left him alone.

"The shoemaker said it couldn't be done to put her in with a corpse. The women started to wail and cross themselves. Then the candlemaker said we should go ahead and do what we said we would do because they were both dead, even if one looked more dead than the other.

"Most of the people agreed with him. Fabrizio, the lamplighter, said it wasn't right to promise Lucia we would bury her with her father and not do it. The promise, after all, contained nothing about the state of her father at the time.

I can see Fabrizio say it! How he loved to sound like a lawyer.

"The women said they should decide because it was a matter of delicacy. Concetta said that if we put her in, she wouldn't recognize her father in that condition. She might think she had been put in with a stranger. To put a young, beautiful, unmarried girl in with a stranger! The women wrung their hands."

Nino lifted his long yellow fingers and pressed his hands together. His nails were stained with iodine; the cuticles seemed to have receded into the fingers, making them look like long and graceful pincers.

"We all stood around in confusion," Nino continued. "The carpenter said, 'I made the coffin for two. Let them rest together.' We all turned to the priest, who had fallen to his knees, praying over the open coffin.

" 'What shall we do, Father? What is the right thing to do now?' we asked him. 'What can be done with them?' "

Nino leaned toward Gina with tears in his eyes. He clasped her hands and fell silent.

"What did the priest say?" Gina asked, breathlessly held by his voice.

"The priest said," Nino continued, " 'Lucia's father had been preserved by God for his goodness. In disturbing his body, we disturbed his rest and his freedom from earthly cares. When he fell into dust, God showed His displeasure at what we had done.' The priest clasped his hands and stared at the skeleton.

"The carpenter said, 'I meant no harm. Madonna mia.'

"Concetta said, 'Father, God sees into our hearts!' and crossed herself.

"The priest said, 'I erred in not preventing this.' " Nino had begun to grin. "He said . . . the priest said . . ."—Nino continued—"he said, 'What is in our hearts has nothing to do with it. Our duty is to follow what has been ordained for us. The right thing is to do what has always been done. *All change is for the worse!'* " Nino was grinning wickedly at Gina.

She stared at him for a moment. "You made that up. You made the whole story up!" She was really mad now, he thought, smiling. He could still catch her up, anytime he wanted. She believed.

"No," he said, smiling. "It was all the truth. Especially the end."

"What end?" Gina demanded. "You never finish anything. You make your own point and let it hang!"

He looked at her, amused. She was really hooked.

"You want to know what they did with the body?"

"Sure," she said, trying to sound cool. "I'm curious. What did they do with it?"

"They argued with the priest for getting them into such a confusing spot. Then they tried to put everything back the way it was before. They nailed up the father's coffin, filled half the double one with flowers, and buried Lucia in it alone. But of course," Nino said in a conciliatory tone, "they couldn't undo what they had done."

Gina watched him.

"Or maybe," Nino continued, "they prayed until God knit back the father's bones and restored his body to its original state."

"Come on," Gina said. "Stop making up stories. I want to know the truth of what they did."

"How you care what I say!" he said. "You thought by walking out, you got out of reach. Well, I can see you didn't. But I'll tell you what happened, just as if you hadn't run away. To tell you the truth," he continued meditatively, "I always wondered whether it was really the best thing they did. Of course, it was the women who believed they had found the answer. Concetta figured out they could wrap the father in a bedspread and pin a picture of him to the top.

This way Lucia would see it was her father. 'Sooner or later,' Concetta said, opening her hands to the sky, 'they will look alike.' She waved to the inscription on the cemetery gate, *'Fummo come voi, sarete come noi.'* As we are now, so you shall be. 'So, it's all right,' Concetta said. I was only a boy, so I didn't give an opinion. But all my life I've wondered."

Gina felt like a small bug caught in a web that spread back into life and forward into death. Which side the spider was on, you wouldn't know until he lunged at you. If you were looking for an out, it didn't pay to try death, because it offered no real exit.

"I've often wondered," Nino repeated, "whether it was really the best thing we did. When I find out, it will clear up a lot. But then it seemed like a simple, practical solution, the kind the women always came up with." He fell silent for what seemed like a long time. Gina, softened by his doubt, wanted to touch his hand. He seemed to sense this, because he reached for hers. "You have to promise me something," he said softly.

Gina nodded, too caught up in the sudden tenderness between them to hedge.

"You foolish little girl," he said gently, brushing her face with his fingers. "Someday you'll see just how foolish you are now. But who knows, it may be a while before I see you again. And when I do I want you to tell me what you've done with yourself. I want you to be able to say that you've always done right."

"But it isn't always possible to tell what the right thing to do is," Gina protested, not liking the direction this was taking. "You yourself just said—"

"If it was easy," Nino interrupted, "it wouldn't be an accomplishment to do it." He tightened his grip, his nails cutting into her wrist.

"Anyway," Gina persisted, "the world out there is different."

She gestured to the window. "It's not so simple. It's not just a question of what you do," she said heatedly. Life with Alex was agony sometimes, because she did do the right thing and it was never enough. "People want more than behavior. They expect . . . they demand a certain kind of feeling going along with it." What a mistake, she felt. She was getting in over her head again. But Nino didn't take advantage.

"We are not sentimental people," Nino said. "Sometimes others don't understand that for us the gesture of respect is love. But it is in . . . personal matters . . . that it makes trouble. Not in other things. It's bad to jump into personal things before you have a clear direction." He looked at her directly. His eyes were filled with pity. "You will jump into everything before you're ready. Your trouble is, you'll never find anything you don't think you're ready for! You're full of curiosity, you're full of desire. You want it all satisfied." But the thought had turned him back toward his rage at her, and he tightened his grip on her hand. "Just remember— you may live differently, you may do this or that, what's right doesn't change. It's always there. You," he said sadly, "just make it harder to find." He could see the tears in her eyes, and he knew the effort she was making not to let them fall. He hadn't wanted to make her cry. He began rubbing the red marks he had made in her wrist. "I'll tell you a secret," he said, leaning toward her.

"What?" she murmured.

"I've always thought they should have buried Lucia alone. A child has to make its own way," he said softly. "If the child finds the right way, it finds its own road back to where it belongs."

His words cut through her. He's releasing me, she thought, as his hands rubbed away the welts.

"I'll tell you something else," Nino said. "So there's at least one other mistake you won't make. Don't look forward to my dying too much. Nothing will be different when I'm dead. Maybe you do know that. I've never been sure what you know. You're deep. Ever since you were a child, you've been deep." He caressed her cheek. "So maybe you know you won't get out of this so easily. You won't get out of this at all." He looked at her kindly, but his interest had clearly flown elsewhere. "Listen, Gina. Be careful. There is no cure for what you've got."

Seven

"Who grows fat, grows beautiful!" said Anna-Maria as she filled her plate. "The sfogliatelli are crispy, the cannoli are creamy. I can never pick which I'm in the mood for." She licked her fingers and settled herself before the coffin. "He looks better now than he did when he was alive. God rest his soul," she said. "He always loved the pastry. That's why I brought it, Nino," she went on, talking to him directly now. "I brought boxes and boxes. And coffee too, but not espresso. Who wants espresso, anyway!" she demanded of him. "It's too bitter. Papa Giuseppe, he never would drink anything else and it ruined his kidneys. And look what it did to yours!"

"He enjoyed it, though," Laura said. Why did Anna-Maria have to bring pastry to his funeral? She had looked through all the funeral parlors in the neighborhood for a really nice place, the kind the young ones wouldn't be embarrassed to come to, and Anna-Maria had to go and make a feast out of the wake. She wasted money on a twenty-cup West Bend pot and all this coffee. Disgusted, Laura helped herself to a butterfly pastry.

What do you expect? Laura appealed to Nino. You never listened to Anna-Maria's problems before. Now, she thought, noting how Anna-Maria was talking comfortably in Nino's ear, you'll have to pay for avoiding her! And to whom besides you could Anna-Maria have told what worried her most. You were the only one she trusted. Since she had cursed her husband and he had died of a heart attack, the vampires she had seen only in her apartment began to appear everywhere. They talked all night, screamed in her ear, tried to take her blood.

Parasites! Anna-Maria said. That's what they are. Just useless, rotten parasites. When she forgot them, she was happy. She did crazy things, but they were happy things. Once she bought a huge birthday cake full of candles and brought it to the old lady next door. Together they had washed it down with beer. She would do generous things when the vampires stayed in their places. But they were always there, she complained to Nino, lurking in toilet bowls. "Maybe now," she was asking him, "now that you are on the other side, Nino, you could tell them to stop bothering me. You are my brother-in-law, Nino," she was reminding him. "You have to do right by me."

"That's right," Laura said to her. "Tell him everything. He has time now." Did his lips twist, Laura wondered, or was it just that every time Anna-Maria opened her mouth he would snarl and get away as quickly as he could? Even in a wheelchair, he could be at the other end of the block as soon as she began to pour out her story. "Pray," he would tell her. "Pray for patience. Pazienza mia!" he would say, and be off. Who did you listen to, Nino, she thought. The neighbors—Malloy who is out of work—him you'd listen to, him you cared about. My own sister who's crazy you didn't have time for. What did you care about her troubles, married to a man forty years older than she? With a limp, no less, when she liked to dance. What did you ever do but think she painted her face too much and cleaned her house too little. It's true, she admitted, but it's no reason for not paying attention.

Laura's eyes filled with tears. She turned to her niece Gloria. "You see your aunt?" she motioned to Anna-Maria. "She's finally getting her chance. God took the wrong sister when he took your mother. She was a wonderful person, Aurelia. How could He have let her die of lung cancer when she never even smoked a cigarette?" Laura shook her head. There is no justice. "This one," she pointed to Anna-Maria, "is just another patient for me. First him," she said, pointing to Nino, "now her. God took the wrong sister," she said again.

"She'll hear you, Aunt Laura," Gloria said. "Don't talk so loud."

"She will drive me crazy," Laura said to Gloria. "Thirty years she lives in a rent-controlled apartment. Three rooms for a hundred and nine dollars a month. All of a sudden to get away from the vampires she packs her bag with her best clothes, pays her rent, puts her keys in the freezer, and leaves a note in the super's mailbox that says, 'Go into my apartment and take what you want. The keys are in the refrigerator.' She leaves her television set, her radio, an expensive clock—things we could have used. She goes to Grand Central Station and gets on a train with no idea where she's going. She gets off when she has to use the bathroom because she thinks the train toilets are dirty. Which," Laura agreed, "they probably are. But where does she end up? New London, Connecticut. Does she know anyone in New London? No! She finds a hotel and I have to go all the way up there and bring her back when her money runs out. She doesn't even have the sense to tell social security where to send her checks. Now she brings food in here and I'll wind up cleaning up the mess."

"It's terrible, Aunt Laura," Gloria agreed. "Maybe there's somewhere she could go. An institution for people like that."

"An institution!" Laura said indignantly. "I can't send her to an institution. She's my sister, even though she's not much company."

Anna-Maria had begun to greet Adela and Cousin Antonetta, who had come in.

"Look," Laura said to Anna-Maria, "I'm the widow, not you."

"You were always jealous of me," Anna-Maria said, smoothing her sweater.

"Me? Jealous of you!" Laura said.

"Of my looks," Anna-Maria said sweetly.

"You look . . . " Laura began, searching for a way to describe a fifty-eight-year-old woman in a miniskirt.

"Don't say it," Adela said. "This is a day of peace. And rest," she said solemnly. "You'll gain an indulgence for putting up with her," she whispered to Laura.

"Eh," Laura said. "Let's forget it." They stood over Nino.

"The flowers make a good showing," Adela said. Huge wreaths ringed the coffin. "This one is from Brother Thomas himself. That one is from the Brothers together."

"That's mine," Laura said, pointing to a heart of red roses. "And the chrysanthemums are from Tommy."

"Tommy? Theresa's boy? The one who's a little . . . " Adela waved her arm.

"Yes," Laura said. "He sent them."

"You wouldn't think someone who lives a strange life like that would remember Nino."

"When you come down to it," Laura said, "he was always a good boy. He still sends money to his mother."

"This is a nice place," said Adela, looking around the room at the carpeting with a pattern of Spanish tiles and the dark Mediterranean furniture.

"I'm glad you like it," Laura said. "Tillie took her father here, so I saw it then and thought it was the best one in the neighborhood."

Adela shook her head. She turned a seasoned gaze on Nino, taking in the silky lining of the coffin.

"He looks very well," Adela said.

"They did a good job," Laura agreed.

"He's not so chalky," Adela noted. They had closed the lower half of the coffin, and it was not apparent that he had no legs.

"I bought that suit for him yesterday, in Robert Hall," Laura said. "The salesman remembered him and found the right size. It fit perfectly on the shoulders. Blue is the best color for him. And I bought the white shirt and tie. Everything's nice and new."

"He looks wonderful," Adela said, taking her hand. Laura had taken care of him for so long, she couldn't stop.

"My deepest sympathy," Vinnie said, taking Laura's free hand. "What a way to go. To have suffered so much and to have put up with everything. That priest they sent for the last rites. When Nino's heart failed, Laura called Our Lady of Perpetual Help to send a priest. They send over this kid to administer the last rites. He was worse than the one who came to Maria. When Nino gets better after they put the pacemaker in—not that they really put it in. He was too weak. So they attached it and let it hang outside. But then his kidneys were not so hot. So when they start to fail, Laura calls for the priest again. Then they fixed that by attaching a bag to his bladder that hangs outside the body. So the next time when the gangrene turned up in his stump, Laura calls the priest again and he says, 'Look, wait a while and call me back when you're sure. It's a cold night.' Cold night!" Vinnie said indignantly. "Some priest. What are they for, if not to make it easier to die? A priest for Bingo nights, that's what he was. And for Nino, who would have crawled, if he had to, to help you out." Vinnie shook his head. "Now there's nobody left from the old neighborhood who remembers. He was a good friend. Appreciated everything you did for him. When he was fourteen and I was only nine, his brother Gabriel—the one he never spoke to—was fighting with him when I came into the house. Gabriel was mean, he had a mean temper. He picked up a kitchen knife. I was only a kid. I knew Gabriel wouldn't cut a kid. I ran between them and said 'Gabriel, what are you doing? Forget it! This is crazy.' He pushed me away, but he throws the knife on the floor and walks out. Nino always thought I saved his life. Or maybe he was grateful that I took it on myself. There was nothing he wouldn't do for me since then. Since I was nine."

"They don't make that kind of gratitude anymore," Adela agreed. "Tell me," she said to Laura. "What did they do with the pacemaker?"

"The pacemaker?"

"Yes. You paid eight hundred dollars for it. And he only used it for a month. What did they do with it when he died?"

They looked at Nino. He wasn't wearing it underneath his new suit.

"What a terrible thing," Laura said. "I never thought of what they did with it. They probably clean it up and sell it again," she said haltingly. "I wouldn't put it past them to do that."

They stood silent in the face of it. "You know," Laura said softly, "I had the fear when I visited Mama before Nino died that the graves were disappearing. She's in an old part of the cemetery and I saw them digging new graves there. But they've been filled up in that section for years. So where could they have gotten the space for new graves? I think they wait to see who gets visitors. And the ones who don't they remove the stones and sell the place again." She shook her head. There was too much to look out for. Nothing was sure, not even after you were gone.

Adela edged closer to Laura. "I have something here I would like to give to Nino," she said, rummaging in her bag. "It's a letter for my sister, Cecilia. I want to send her my regards and to tell her I am taking care of the plants she left and I keep an eye on her son. She was always worried about how he eats, and I want her to know I have him for supper at least once or twice every week."

Laura nodded. Adela tucked the letter deep in Nino's coffin. Around them came the others, the ones who only came out for weddings and funerals, the ladies in black, oldest of the relatives, one of them over ninety, but still getting around. They gathered around Nino; some gave notes; others asked for favors.

Would he remember all this? Laura wondered. Even when he was asked to pick up a quart of milk he would forget. Would he give Adela's regards to Cecilia and carry all the messages poured into his ear? Could he do Anna-Maria any good over there? He would have to, she concluded. It was his responsibility now.

Gina was standing back, half concealed by the chrysanthemum wreath. Her hair had grown much longer, Laura noticed. She had pulled it back and twisted it into a knot. Laura could see her watching the old ladies talking to Nino, munching pastry, tucking letters under his arm. It's so much easier, Gina thought, if you could send a message like that. Then you could get across what you meant; if you put it in writing there would be no mistake about the meaning. The sight of the heavy custard pastries was somehow reassuring.

He does look better now than when he was alive, Gina saw. The thought of his life gripped her more painfully than his death. To sicken in pieces, one limb at a time, one function lost after another. Even his eyes were going. She could see him still in the last hospital he had gone to. Not a good hospital, just one nearby so it was easy to visit. If they help him anymore, Laura had said, he'll die faster! How much help could he take? First the transplant, then the amputations, then the pacemaker, then the insertion of the tube and bag. It was too terrible, one trauma crowding another. As the year stretched deep into winter, there was less and less of him left. And yet he had been able to turn away from his decline, even as she turned from him.

Near the end he had ceased to speak English. He murmured in the dialect of his town. He seemed politely irritated if anyone came in, as if he had been interrupted in a conversation more interesting than any a visitor could offer. He had only once reached out to her. His long fingers had stretched toward her. The tips, she thought, were blackish. Maybe his hands would have gone next—the words crowded her mind. But he was bent on making a final point. "When I see you again," he had repeated, "I don't want to hear the same stupid remarks you always make. Do the right thing!"

"What is it?" she whispered.

"Go figure it out," he said.

"It's not the kind of thing you can figure out. Either you know or you don't know."

"If you don't know," Nino said, "don't bother coming around. If there's one thing I can't stand, it's a confused person."

"If there's one thing I can't stand," Gina said, "it's a person who gives confusing advice."

"You see," Nino said, "we agree on everything." He reached for her hand. "I don't mind emotion, you know. I'm not afraid of feeling."

It was so much easier to argue with him than not. I really failed you, Nino, Gina thought. I really blew it! You gave me one last chance to say . . . to say what? I love you. It would have been so unlike everything we had been to each other to say that. But the time, the place, everything cried out for something different. There is no way, Nino, she thought, no way I didn't fail you by saying what I said. If I could send a note, she thought, maybe I wouldn't say "I forgot to tell you I loved you." But I could say something else. I still can't think what. Maybe just apologize for making dumb jokes, for shutting you up. The idea of a letter, she thought wistfully, wasn't bad.

"My deepest sympathy," Angelo said to her.

She looked at him for a moment, coming back from her thoughts all too slowly. "What did you say?" she asked, smiling slightly at him.

"My deepest sympathy," he repeated sheepishly. "When in Rome," he began, letting the sentence trail off. "I'm sorry about Nino," Angelo said. "Really sorry. He was one of a kind."

Gina grinned at him. "Yes, he was."

"They don't make them like that anymore."

"No," she agreed, "they don't."

"It's probably just as well," he ventured. "I hear you're on your own now."

"Yes," she said. "I was at an SRO hotel for a while, but now I'm moving to my own apartment. You have to come and see."

"Where is it?"

"MacDougal Street. It has a tub in the kitchen, but a private bathroom and a fireplace. And it's cheap." The thought of the apartment cheered her. She was full of plans for it. After months at the Bristol, she had come to hate the long corridors, the dingy kitchen, the moldy refrigerator, the stove that seemed constantly visited by mice.

"Aren't you moving back with Laura now that she's alone?" Angelo asked.

"Maybe I'll stay with her for a while."

"It agrees with you to be on your own?" Angelo asked.

"It does." Gina said. "Sometimes I wake up in the morning and look around and I feel . . . blessed . . . just to be there, just to be away."

"You must be in love," Angelo offered.

Gina looked at him. He knows about Alex, she thought, but he isn't going to say. Neither am I. Alex had been willing to come, but she had told him not to. He had been so loving. He had woken up early with her that morning and brewed a huge pot of tea against the chill of his room. She could feel him still, feel the wash of tenderness he poured with his arms, his kiss, his thighs winding around her. Sometimes he could be perfect. And then others he seemed to generate the most intense restlessness in her. Once you move out, she had realized, you keep moving out. It's not something you want to stop. Maybe that's what Nino meant by a disease: the moving disease. The way the world looks to you is how you know you've got it. To me, Gina thought, it looks like a train I absolutely must get on.

"Are you?" Angelo pressed.

"What?" she said absently.

"In love."

Gina shrugged. "Do you want some sfogliatelli?" she asked. "I'm really hungry for one."

Laura watched them thank Aunt Anna-Maria for the pastries. Vinnie was praying on his knees beside the coffin. Coming toward them were four boys in motorcycle jackets. What a disgrace! Motorcycle jackets! They must be boys he once worked with, she realized, softening. Vinnie, finishing his prayers, seemed to know them. Adela was offering them coffee. Maybe, Laura thought, Anna-Maria was right to bring pastry after all. Maybe, she sighed, the old ways are best. The young ones are eating too, and they don't seem to mind.

Father Romano touched her shoulder. "It's time to begin," he said.

"I'm glad you could come and say the prayer," Laura said warmly.

Vinnie patted Romano on the back. "Nino wouldn't have wanted anyone but you." As Father Romano signaled for silence, everyone found a seat. Vinnie whispered to Laura, "At least we got rid of Bingo Benny."

They found seats, Gina and Vinnie next to Laura, Angelo sitting just behind Gina.

"We are gathered here to honor the memory of our brother Nino, who passed from among us. Let us remember that as surely as he has gone before us, so shall we follow after. So let us celebrate the goodness of his life as a loyal son of the Church, ever mindful that the death of each of us is an example for all. It has been said that in striking our hearts, death only stirs up the embers of our faith. We are stricken in our loss, we shudder because we do not fully comprehend the Lord. Insofar as we are not like Him, we can only be pained. But if we have the divine spark within us, we may feel whatever wisdom flickers through us and mirrors our knowledge of God. The effort of our brother Nino was to turn from distractions from the Lord even as he lived in the world. He did his best to keep his eyes upon the ways of the Lord, in offering his help and wisdom and guidance to those young people who needed it.

"As Saint Augustine has written: 'Be not conformed to this world . . . but cultivate a thirst for the spiritual nourishment of the church which is the world as it was, and live in a vision of God's world.' As God forgives our iniquities, so he heals all infirmities."

"He was a little slow in helping Nino out with the gangrene," Angelo whispered.

Gina waved his words away. She was, Angelo saw, swallowing it all. "Hey," he whispered, "with your hair pulled back and all in black you look like the real thing. You could have walked in off the streets of Palermo."

"Shut up," Gina said. She had missed some of Father Romano's words.

" . . . affliction befell him, but his faith withstood the pressure of disease and amputation. The Lord redeems life from corruption; he has redeemed our brother now. We know that Christ died for all, that they who live may now no longer live unto and for themselves, but unto Him that died for them. There is no final joy in the material world," Father Romano said firmly. "Therefore, the degrees of suffering we face fall away in the experience of grace, in the recognition of the infinite and sustaining perfection of the soul with God."

"This isn't a prayer for the dead, it's a filibuster," said Angelo. "Why didn't you get Father Moran?" he demanded of Vinnie. "He gets it over with in a few minutes."

Vinnie was mad. You could say what you like about Romano, but when you were in a spot, he came through. He was a real priest. "If you say one more word," he hissed to Angelo, "you'll be next!"

Angelo fell silent. All around him, the relatives were lapping it up. Even Gina looked like she couldn't get enough of old Romano. He studied her profile, finely shaped nose, high cheekbones. She seemed completely self-possessed, at peace. It hit him. Now that Nino was gone, she had gone back to him! No wonder he felt alone.

Romano had passed on to other things. "Augustine also teaches us that 'there is no soundness in them, whom aught of Thy creation displeaseth.' "

"Lots of things displeased Nino," Laura murmured, with tears in her eyes. Gina reached for her hand.

" . . . so is our salvation," Father Romano continued,

heedless of less than perfect attention, "in discovering the light that dwells among the shadows, lurking even in darkness as a beacon of God's grace. Our brother, though a sinner—as are we all!—was ever mindful that repentance opened up the way to the Lord. In the Lord is reconciled our hope for eternity and our fear of life and death, our sin and our longing for grace, the imperfect flesh which makes us shudder at the hand of God and the divine soul which makes us gleam, even through our misfortune.

"In understanding the death of our brother, we must try to understand its meaning for our lives. Our everlasting teacher, Saint Augustine, tells us that 'virtue is the good use of free choice.' Those who live in the world must perfect the good that we associate with action. By what you do, you can demonstrate your kinship with God. This goodness is open to each and every one of us, no matter what our calling, no matter how humble. Every act of virtue, Saint Thomas tells us, can be done from choice. But nothing makes us choose rightly except that part of the soul that wishes to be felt in the world, in action.

"Will we choose what is moral or what is ill? How can we acquire the habit of morality? We are here"—Father Romano's eyes had begun to fill—"at the spot that I can best remember brother Nino, not as a priest but as a boyhood friend."

"They used to talk a lot," Vinnie whispered to Gina. "When they were in school, Papa Joe, Nino's father, would take them for a Marsala and they would stay talking . . . "

Father Romano was losing his priestly tone. "We are beset now by a time when our moral discipline is severely strained. Our Church is our refuge in this storm." He paused, his mind lingering over the past. "When we were boys, we wrestled with the questions people have always wrestled with when they look at the world and find it full of iniquity, inhumanity, cruelty. But," he continued, almost pleadingly, "what individual in one lifetime can arrive at the right answers? An answer cannot be an answer for the moment, a solution only of a day. It must be an answer for all time."

"What is this, one of those Protestant preachers you got us, Vinnie?" Angelo whispered.

Vinnie brought his heel back smartly into Angelo's ankle.

"No virtue," Romano went on, "makes us choose rightly. We must have the will to be right, to accept the gift of God's grace."

"You see!" Angelo hissed.

"Our blessing is the recognition that the Church has understood and perfected this will, and translated much of it for us into guidelines in the art of right conduct."

Vinnie nodded emphatically; he had his own guidelines.

"Our brother Nino prayed for vigilance and for strength in his efforts on behalf of the misguided Catholic boys in his care. Now it is for us to be vigilant for the welfare of our souls, for who among us knows who will be called next before the Lord." Father Romano paused and raised his hand dramatically. "Let us pray," he said.

When the soothing, familiar prayers had been said and the benediction given, Father Romano took a drink.

"The hand that makes the sign of the cross is still the first to grab the vino, eh," said Angelo, slapping the priest on the back.

"No wonder you get so dry, talking so much," Vinnie said, ignoring Angelo.

Father Romano shrugged and sipped.

"Now there's no one who was part of the old days," Father Romano said hoarsely. "All the others have moved somewhere else or departed this world."

"I know what you mean," Vinnie said.

"Gone," Angelo commented, "but not forgotten."

Vinnie gave him a warning look. Nino was right. The kid

was trouble. If there's one thing that doesn't belong at a funeral, he thought, it's sarcasm.

Gina pulled Angelo away.

"What's bothering you?" she said. "You really are impossible. Nobody behaved like that at your mother's funeral."

"That's what bothers me. Funerals, period. Do you know how many I've been to in my life? And I'm only twenty-five. Since I was in the first grade at Our Lady of Perpetual Help, I've been to every funeral of every relative of every kid in the school. Especially since ninety-nine percent of them were across the street at Murdock's funeral home. Other kids had recess and played baseball. We crossed ourselves in front of corpses. I must have put in several thousand hours smelling rooms full of death and roses. Everybody was great at my mother's funeral," he agreed. "But me, I was keeping it all in."

"Why didn't you say anything?"

"What could I say?" he said evasively.

"It was Nino, wasn't it?" she demanded. "He did something that kept you in line. What did he do?" she asked curiously. He couldn't have taken a strap to Angelo; he was too big.

"What did he do? Come on, tell me." Gina pressed him, smiling.

"You'll never find out from me," Angelo said. "Just make me a promise."

"What?"

"When I die, don't show up at my funeral and say 'my deepest sympathy' to anybody. Don't let Aunt Anna-Maria ask me to kill the vampires from the other side. And tell Concetta I couldn't care less if Cecilia knows her plants are being watered every day, and tell—"

Gina laughed. "Didn't you hear Father Romano? What makes you think that your death gives you any say?" She smiled wryly. "You don't die for yourself, you die for all of us, just as you live for them and not for yourself. That's it," she said. "That's the deal."

Angelo looked at her. He didn't think it was funny.

"Look," she continued, shaking her head. "Look how ridiculous we are. I can't avoid putting up with you and you can't stop complaining. Look at my mother," she said, pointing to Laura. "She is completely self-possessed. She took care of him day and night, supported him, and watched over everything from the first moment of his illness. Do you think she feels disturbed? She's sorry he's dead, but her life"—she poked him in the chest—"is in order. It's a perfect balance sheet. Every responsibility has been discharged. She won't even be lonely for more than a little while. She'll take up the care of Aunt Anna-Maria, draw up a new slate, and balance that too. That's the way they are."

"It's not the way I am. I can't take the rigidity of it. Not that Aunt Laura's rigid. But the whole robot life, one thing after another . . ." He shook his head in disgust.

"I know," she agreed. "It's awful. But they don't think it's awful. We just don't see it the same way. But it doesn't pay to be bitter and angry about it." She hadn't been angry, really angry, she realized suddenly, since she had left. There were other problems, but not that leaden rage, not that sense that they were coming for her. She looked back at the coffin. She had seen it before, somewhere. Somewhere it had been coming fast, coming for her. But that seemed like a thousand years ago.

"They'll be closing soon," Angelo said. Irritating as it was here, he didn't want to go home. His eye caught Cousin Vinnie's. "Now you're the head man," he joked.

Vinnie shook his head. "He was the last. At least in this family."

It was true, Angelo thought. Vinnie really didn't have whatever it took.

208 · *Josephine Gattuso Hendin*

Hey, Nino, Gina thought. She could hear everyone saying goodbye. Tomorrow they would bury him and it wouldn't be the same. *"Saludama Cecilia!"* Adela was saying.

"You'll never find anyone who cared for you the way he did," Vinnie said.

"No," Gina said. "I won't." Somehow, talking to Angelo had killed the impulse to say "Good!"

"I'm leaving now," Angelo said. "I'll take Aunt Anna-Maria home."

"You'll gain an indulgence," Gina whispered, grinning.

"I'll say goodbye now," Angelo said. "I'm not coming to the cemetery tomorrow."

"OK," Gina said. "Thanks for coming tonight." She watched for a minute as he packed up Aunt Anna-Maria's twenty-cup electric coffee pot. She could see the funeral parlor people in the wings, waiting to close up. She knew they were closing up Nino too! Hey, Nino, she thought, seeing all the letters tucked in around him, no rest for the weary! When I see you again, I want you to be able to tell me you delivered all your letters.

"You know," Laura said apologetically, "it's just the old custom. I had no idea so many people would be letter-writers!" She looked embarrassed.

"It's OK," Gina said. "It's not a bad custom."

"I never thought you would say that."

"There's nothing wrong with it."

"Do you think he'll remember to deliver them?" Laura asked hesitantly.

"He has plenty of time to do the job."

"He never even remembered if I asked him to get bread and milk."

"This is different," Gina said.

"Sometimes, you know, you even receive answers. I saw Camilla last month when I was asleep. Did I tell you?"

"No," Gina said. "What did she say?"

"She asked me to look out for Gloria and make sure she doesn't get too thin. Do you think it was real, or do you think it was just a dream? Those things don't happen here. You know, my mother once went to the fountain to fill her jug with water for the house. She was there, filling it, when all of a sudden she saw another woman pouring water over her hands. 'Marcellina, hello!' she called out, and the other woman smiled sadly. Then she remembered the woman had died three months before, and she said 'Jesus, Mary, and Joseph' and crossed herself. As soon as she did that, the woman vanished. But that was in the old country, where people were superstitious. Even the priests. Your father used to tell that when he was a boy he heard of an eruption of Mount Aetna. The earth blew open just above the town of Nicolosi. The lava poured out like a river of fire. But the priests came from Catania with a relic of Saint Agatha. They held it up before the lava and you know what?"

"What?" Gina said.

"The lava stopped. Now who can say for sure whether the lava stopped for Saint Agatha or whether it just stopped? Down there," Laura said, referring to Sicily, "they overdo it. They have a Day of the Dead in November. The second of November, I think. The Giorno dei Morti is bigger than Christmas. They give all the kids big presents in the names of the dead in the family. It's just the way things are done . . . were done. Now things may be different, even there. Now they have running water," she said, thinking of her mother's huge well jar.

Gina drew back as she saw Laura turn to kiss Nino goodbye. She has never been bitter, Gina thought, watching her. No matter what he did, or how they fought, she has never turned sour. Gina felt a rush of tenderness for her mother. It would have been so easy for Laura to try to make her feel guilty, to ask her to move back. But she had done neither.

They walked out together into the winter night.

"Get in, we've been waiting for you," Vinnie said from his overpacked car. "I'm taking everybody home." They made room for Laura and for Gina.

"No thanks," Gina said. "Nobody's going my way, it's too far in the other direction. I'll get a cab." She closed the door after Laura.

"Don't take the train alone at this hour," Laura said. "I'll see you here tomorrow. Don't forget! Eight o'clock sharp."

"I'll be here," Gina promised, watching the car pull away. She walked down the street toward the subway station, feeling less tired with every step. The silvery clouds stretching here and there couldn't dim the brilliant full moon. A white light seemed to flood the streets, brightening the tinsel on discarded Christmas trees still waiting to be picked up. It was only ten o'clock, but the streets were empty except for isolated figures hurrying along.

After so much noise, Gina thought, what a wonderful silence. The air was shockingly cold after the flower-choked room. She ignored the cab that passed, unwilling to give up the sensation of the sharp air, the white light. At the subway station, she turned left without hesitating, and kept walking. There was a time, she thought, when I hated this walk. Under the El, soot always sifted down into your eyes, your hair, your clothes. But the winter wind was pure, cold, dustless. She could remember waiting for buses—was it only five or six months ago?—when she stood in a dirt shower while the screeching train wheels cut into her ears like knives. Now the wind blew the noise away.

She had always thought Queens Plaza had to be one of the ugliest places on earth. She could see Long Island City High School off to the right, circled by a parking lot, two crumbling factories, and a pizza place. It must be something in me, she realized, because I don't feel pulled by these things anymore. The noise doesn't reach me; the street is just to walk on; I can't lay hold of the four years I spent in the school with the blackened windows. The traffic pressing around her as she made her way to the walkway of the Queensboro Bridge only made the night sing. She kept moving forward, climbing over the chain that closed off the walkway, rushing up the ascent.

The moon washed the river in white light. Here and there bits of ice were floating like flat arrows on the shimmering water. In the distance, the Empire State Building, still lit red and green from Christmas, anchored the city, the curving edge of waterfront winding south from it. Cars and lights colored the river's edge as far as she could see. The wind over the water was searing, but she didn't bother to zip her jacket. She stumbled; riveted on the city floating in the river, floating in space, she didn't notice the metal rubble on the walkway. The path was an obstacle course of old junk: mufflers shiny with grease, old cans, bridge-beams feathered with flaking paint. A bridge like a ruin, she thought, brushing flakes of rust from her skirt, a ruin like a bridge. The surface was worn down to the metal supports; it gleamed in the moonlight from sheer use, the metal bones of a breaking back.

From here she could see it all: the great skyline, curving north and south, set off by the dark water, the shiny river reflecting light into the clear, cold night. The wind was dizzying, intoxicating; it was lifting her out of herself. All her life she had been afraid of the odds against her, but her wariness was gone, lost somewhere in the bright night. "Nino. Nino," she whispered into the cold, "someday I'll write you a letter." But it was the bridge arching, the white wind soaring, the chilling purity that made the night right.

The Right Thing to Do

has been set on the Linotron 202 in Baskerville, a fine transitional typeface designed about 1760 by the English printer John Baskerville. A controversial face which originally found more favor on the Continent than in England, Baskerville did not win popular acceptance until its recutting by the Monotype Corporation in 1923. Since then this widely used face has been adapted to use on the Linotype and for photocomposition. A round, open typeface, it is characterized by thin hairlines, slightly bracketed serifs, and generous proportions.
Composition by PennSet, Inc., Bloomsburg, Pennsylvania. Printed and bound by the Haddon Craftsmen, Scranton, Pennsylvania. Design by Virginia Evans.